DEMON SUMMER

Demon Summer

J.J. BUFFET

A SNAXTIME ORIGINAL CHILLER

Brooklyn, NY

SNAXTIME
www.snaxtime.com

ISBN: 979-8-9914890-0-3

Edited by Adrienne Kisner
Additional proofreading by Elizabeth Thurmond
Cover art by Jamie Dwyer & Justin Ulloa

"There is a touch of magic behind every great dish."

— Harold Snaxton, Founder of Snaxtime, 1949

PROLOGUE

300 YEARS AGO

"Don't linger too long in the forest," Henry's mother warned him. Her eyes darted toward the woods that encircled their home.

"There's no need to worry, Mother," he assured her.

She gripped his hands. "The baker's lad and the blacksmith's apprentice are still missing... It's not safe."

"I will be back in no time."

For Henry, the forest was like a second home. He had explored its depths on numerous adventures with his younger sister, Abigail. But she was now confined to her bed, weakened by a fever that had gripped her for days.

Together, they had found a secret spot in the woods where the sweetest strawberries grew in plenty. Today, Henry would go fetch some and bring them back to his sister. Paired with the biscuits his mother had made that morning, they would surely comfort Abigail's ailing heart.

He set off into the forest with an empty basket. Spears of morning light pierced through the trees overhead. His sun-bleached hair shone like straw. Days toiling in the fields had left his skin tanned and his lanky frame hardened with muscle. At 18 years of age, he was a striking young man.

Henry reached the patch. The strawberries were ripe and plump. He plucked one, savoring its tangy sweetness before gathering more into his basket.

He heard a playful rustling, followed by high-pitched giggling. The sounds resembled woodland sprites at play, frolicking among the trees and ferns. Curiosity overtook caution as he abandoned his task to discover the source of the mysterious noises.

Then a different sound filtered through the trees—a mesmerizing song. The voice was otherworldly in its beauty. Spellbound, Henry found himself walking deeper into the forest.

The farther he wandered, the louder and more intoxicating the song became. The forest blurred around him as the music overwhelmed his senses.

He arrived upon a secluded pool, its turquoise waters fed by a cascading waterfall. Water lilies dotted the surface.

In the heart of the oasis was an exquisite maiden. Her black hair fell in a waterfall of its own down her buxom figure. Her supple skin was as pale as moonlight, her lips the color of roses. Her eyes were clear as ice. She opened her arms, welcoming him into her naked bosom.

Entranced, Henry dropped the basket and shed his clothes. He slipped into the pool and waded toward the heavenly creature. The water, warm like fresh milk, excited him.

Swimming forward, he didn't notice that something was trailing behind him. Suddenly, sharp grips clamped onto his ankles and yanked him below the surface.

He thrashed to break free. His frantic eyes begged the maiden for help. Yet she observed him with unsettling tranquility.

The water suddenly froze over with unnatural speed, trapping him under a sheath of ice. He pounded the barrier above, but his strength faded within the freezing tomb.

The woman appeared underwater, gliding with predatory grace toward him. Her blue eyes glowed in the icy abyss.

As she drew closer, her lips parted to reveal a grotesque sight—rows of jagged, shark-like teeth that betrayed her beauty.

Above the surface, the serene pool underwent a ghastly transformation. Its blue waters turned red beneath the ice. The gushing waterfall suspended mid-cascade, frozen.

Nearby, Henry's basket was left behind, its juicy strawberries spilled out around it, never to be tasted.

CHAPTER ONE

Zane Hawthorn poked at the soggy bat-shaped marshmallows in his bowl of Ghoulie Crunch Cereal—his childhood favorite. The chocolate crunchies were still "ghoulishly delicious," as advertised.

The last several months had been pretty crazy. It all started with a letter he received on Christmas Day. Apparently, some great-uncle named Reginald—whom Zane had never heard of—had died of old age. The letter came with the deed to a small house in a town called Paradise Falls, and the news that Zane was the last surviving member of a family he knew nothing about. As an orphan, it was a really weird way to learn about his roots.

He had just graduated high school and moved into the house a few days ago. Starting over in a new town was daunting, but finding a job came easy.

The day he moved in, he got a random text message that he almost ignored as spam. It advertised a job at Snaxtime, a fast-food chain he'd always been a fan of—those Cheesy Tots were the stuff of legend. He'd never worked in a restaurant before, but the manager didn't seem to care; his laid-back charm and genuine love for fast food sealed the deal. The gig had basically fallen into his lap—it felt like fate. Today, he would join their ranks, marking his next step toward independence.

As he got ready for his first day, Zane studied himself in his bedroom mirror. His blue eyes were almost clear, a feature that people often commented on. Tattoos were scattered across his arms, chest, and neck. He collected them like charms on a bracelet. He slipped his uniform over his head and brushed back a rebellious lock of jet-black hair.

Here goes nothing.

Zane stepped out of his house, skateboard in hand. He hopped on and made his way to Snaxtime. Here in Paradise Falls, maybe he'd finally discover who he was meant to be.

Snaxtime was a yellow brick building on a hill overlooking the city. Its upswept red roof was crowned with a giant neon hot dog.

The Snaxtime franchise had been delighting customers since the late 1940s, when its founder, Harold Snaxton, opened a humble hot dog shack in Paradise Falls. The small business was an immediate success, expanding nationally to hundreds of locations over the next several decades. While the original building had been renovated several times over the years, it was still touted as the birthplace of the Original Cheese Dog.

Zane stepped inside. The aroma of sizzling hot dogs and fried food welcomed him to his new job. The interior was a riot of color, with bright orange and blue plastic booths lining the walls. Murals showcased cartoon food characters with smiling faces. There were plenty of workers bustling behind the counter and in the kitchen, but it was the bubbly redhead at the register who grabbed his attention.

"You must be the new victim." She extended her hand. Her acrylic nails gleamed like cherry candies under the fluorescent lights. "I'm Star." She gave a playful wink, her freckled nose crinkling. A pink bubble of gum popped between her lips. "The pleasure is totally *yours*."

Star's tight uniform accentuated her curvy frame. Smiley face earrings dangled from her ears. Zane liked her fun and flirty vibe. He could see himself enjoying her company.

"Ha, nice to meet you too," he replied, shaking her hand. "Zane."

A wiry young man eagerly bounded over and greeted Zane with a smirk. "Hi, I'm Dexter." His curly dark hair was piled high, clipped down to a fade. He pushed up his glasses. "Welcome to Snaxtime, where dreams come to *fry*." He flashed a wide, gap-toothed grin.

"What's up, Dex?" Zane chuckled. Dexter looked like an adorable comic-book character.

"Hey, lemme tell you about the time…"

"Alright, Dexter, that's enough," interrupted an older woman, who Zane recognized as Marjorie, the manager who had interviewed him on Zoom. "Don't get Dexter started with his stories. Trust me, you'll be here 'til next week!"

Dexter grinned, "Marjorie, you've just deprived Zane of the tale of the century."

The woman turned to Zane. "Welcome, Mr. Hawthorn. Nice to meet ya in person!"

"Thanks, I'm excited to be here."

Marjorie wasn't tall, but she had a presence. Her strawberry-blonde hair was streaked with white, giving her a kind of quirky charm. Despite years of wear, her Snaxtime uniform was still vibrant and perfectly pressed.

"Let's get you started on your training."

For several hours, Zane was thrown headfirst into the busy world of Snaxtime. Marjorie, making everything seem easy, showed him the ropes of their fast-food operations. He learned how to use the cash registers and manage the flow of orders from both drive-thru and in-store customers, keeping everything moving smoothly.

Then there were the finer points—restocking supplies without interrupting the workflow, the ideal temperature for the creamiest soft-serve ice cream, and the routine of arranging the dining area to meet Snaxtime's clean and inviting standards.

Marjorie's voice took on a softer, more reflective tone in a brief lull following the afternoon rush. Her eyes lingered on the familiar surroundings—the counter she'd operated countless times, the kitchen where she'd honed her skills, the register that had initially seemed daunting. "You know, Zane," she began, her words steeped in nostalgia and pride, "I started working here at Snaxtime when I was just 16. Can you believe that?"

Zane poured a bucket of ice into a bin. "Wow! So, you just started here last week?" he asked playfully.

"Very funny, Zane. I'm probably old enough to be your grandma!"

Zane chuckled. "So, why stick around so long?"

"Oh, you know, lots of things. This place is so special. You can just feel its energy. I swear, there's magic in the air. And I've made so many memories here. Mostly good ones. Aaaand some not-so-good ones, too!"

"Like what?"

"Like when we first added Jalapeño Hot Bites to the menu. Boy, was that a day! We were all so excited we must've eaten a hundred of 'em each." She placed her hand on her round belly. "And wow, lemme tell ya, those bathrooms have never been the same since!"

Zane laughed. "Sounds like a real *blast!*"

"You could definitely say that!" Marjorie placed a Snaxtime cap on Zane's head, "Okay, you're up, rookie. Time to start your own Snaxtime adventure."

She led him to the kitchen, advising cheerfully, "Remember, clean apron, bright smile. You're going to rock this. Now, let's move on to the grill." She motioned to a young man brimming with confidence and charisma. "Zane, this is Jake. He'll show you how to make all of our sandwiches. You're in good hands with him." Marjorie left.

Jake's muscular frame, snug in his uniform, was complemented by a healthy tan. Wavy blond hair topped his head, and his smile gleamed white. He wore a trendy pearl necklace.

Zane fist-bumped his new colleague. "Yo, I'm diggin' the pearls."

"Thanks. Fresh, right?" Jake touched his neck. "Some rando company sent it to me for doing a sponsored post on social. Oh, what's your handle?" He pulled out his phone.

"Um, I'm not very active on social."

"Don't sweat it. Everybody's gotta start somewhere. You've got the look, dude. Hang with me, and you'll be blowing up in no time," Jake promised.

"Sounds good." Zane had no actual interest in being an influencer, but he appreciated the offer.

"So, let's get things fired up," Jake said, flipping a burger patty from spatula to bun.

Jake was a good teacher. With expert flair, he guided Zane through each menu item, complete with his seasoning tips and grill tricks.

After a thorough demo, Jake handed Zane a pair of tongs. "Now, you give it a try. Let's start with what we're known for — the Cheesy Double Dog."

First, Zane pulled a toasted bun from the warming drawer and tucked a plump dog inside. This wasn't your everyday wiener, it was a decadent cheese-stuffed delight. He moved it under a sauce dispenser and crowned it with an artful spiral of bright yellow cheese. It looked perfect.

"Beautiful!" Jake proclaimed. "Insta-worthy, for sure."

Zane worked his way through the Classic Fish Deluxe, Grilled Cheese, and Double Cheeseburger. Then came the Snaxtime Supreme. This quadruple-patty burger was the Mount Everest of fast food. It took a lot of careful stacking to keep the skyscraper from tumbling down. Layer by layer, Zane alternated between beef and cheese before adding bacon, lettuce, tomato, pickles, onion, ketchup, mustard, mayo, and cheese sauce.

"I think I'm getting the hang of this." Zane looked up from assembling the colossal sandwich. "It's almost as tall as you!" he joked. Jake towered over him, easily hitting 6'5.

With Zane's eyes distracted, the sandwich started to topple over. Jake jumped in, using his swift reflexes to steady it and wrap it expertly in one fluid motion.

"Whoa, spoke too soon. Looks like I could use a little more practice," Zane admitted with a sheepish grin.

Jake winked. "Don't worry, I gotchu."

Free lunch at Snaxtime was a top perk, and Zane was ready to eat. He settled into a corner booth with a Cheesy Double Dog, Cheesy Stix, and an Orange Gush soda.

Zane inhaled his food with gusto. He'd been going to Snaxtime since he could remember. But there was a certain magic about the original location that made the food even better.

He was about to get up to resume training when Star, Jake, and Dexter came over. They were each carrying a tray piled high with various menu items.

Dexter's thick glasses magnified his puppy-dog eyes. "Ready for your hazing, or should I say *grazing?*"

Star rolled her eyes. "Do you, like, study a dad joke book before bed every night?"

Zane looked at the intimidating trays of food and laughed. "What's all this?"

"It's tradition," Star responded. "On your first day, you have to sample everything."

"Well, not *everything,*" Dexter clarified. "We don't want to kill you off right away."

Jake pushed the trays closer to Zane. "There's only one way to *really* learn the menu. Dig in!"

Zane wasn't sure how much he could eat, but he'd try his best to impress the crew. "Bring it!"

First on the tasting itinerary was the Cheesy Corn Dog. The sweet, crunchy batter provided a delightful contrast to the cheese-filled meat within. As Zane bit into it, he relished the satisfying crunch and gooey cheese.

Next, Zane tried the Grilled Cheese. The bread was perfectly toasted, buttery and crisp, with hot, velvety cheese oozing out. Each bite was warmly familiar.

Then came the Jalapeño Hot Bites. They were spicy, with a crunchy outside and a cheddar-flavored filling that balanced the heat.

The Cheesy Tots, already one of Zane's favorites, were perfect little bites topped with cheese. Each had a golden crust on the outside and a soft, warm potato center. He made quick work of them, one by one.

The Crunchy Beef Tacos were next. Inside the crispy shells was a generous serving of spicy ground beef topped with shredded lettuce, tomatoes, and sharp cheddar. They might've been the best tacos he'd ever had.

The Pineapple Party Cake was a sweet tropical finish. The light sponge cake was filled with juicy pineapple chunks and topped with vanilla frosting, a pineapple slice, shredded coconut, and a cherry. The cake was indeed a party for his palate.

Zane took one last slurp of his soda and pushed the trays away from him. He discreetly unbuttoned his pants for relief. *Ugh.* He felt sick. "How'd I do, guys?"

"Wow, Zane," Star said. "We didn't think you'd, like, *actually* be able to eat everything."

Jake added, "Yeah, you're giving Dexter a run for his money!"

"Pfft, I could do that in half the time," Dexter countered, leaning back as he stretched his arms behind his head. "Did I ever tell you guys about the time I became the Cheese Dog King at the Paradise Falls Carnival?"

"Um, like a *million* times." Star was already annoyed.

Unfazed, Dexter continued, "No one thought I'd ever stand a chance, you see. There was this big shot, Gordy the Gobbler, a twenty-year reigning champ. Picture a guy the size of a pickup truck, arms like tree trunks, who could down a dozen cheese dogs a minute. That was Gordy.

"I was the underdog, literally. A mere Snaxtime fry cook with a dream. We faced off on the main stage with Miss Paradise Falls herself, the lovely Patsy Peterson, a true local celebrity, as our judge. She wore this sash and tiara with a red, white, and blue bikini. It was awesome. And the crowd, they loved Gordy. To them, I was just a sideshow.

"But man, did I show them! I kept up with Gordy, bite for bite. You could hear the gasps from the audience each time I finished a dog. With every cheesy chomp, their disbelief grew. We had each downed 34 dogs and had less than a minute to go. I could see Gordy faltering.

"That's when it happened." Dexter let out a laugh, shaking his head at the memory. "On my final victorious bite, a perfect jet of cheese sauce squirted out of my dog. It shot through the air, and—I swear I couldn't have planned this—it landed right on Patsy's... Let's say 'décolletage.'" Dexter was a polished storyteller.

He continued, "The crowd went silent. You could've heard a popcorn kernel drop. Then the mayor's dog, Bingo, spotted the cheese and, well, dogs will be dogs. He saw his opportunity and took it, jumping up on Patsy for a taste. Poor woman, she shrieked, stumbled backward, and reached out to steady herself. The only thing to hold on to was the tablecloth."

Dexter's story climaxed with him laughing, barely able to get the words out. "She pulls the tablecloth out from under everything, and it's like the Fourth of July! Hot dogs flying in every direction. Chaos, absolute chaos!

"But here's the kicker," Dexter wiped a tear of laughter from his eye, "In all that commotion, nobody noticed me swallowing that last bite. By the time the dust had settled, Gordy was one dog short of a tie, and I was crowned the Cheese Dog King!"

Star's hands came together in a sarcastic, slow clap. "Did you hear that, Zane? You're dining in the royal presence of the one-and-only Cheese Dog *King*."

Jake laughed along. "Oh man, that story gets better every time I hear it."

"Does it, though?" Star said under her breath.

Jake gave Dexter a high five. "That Bingo is one lucky *DAWG!*"

As Zane coasted through the final tasks of his shift, Star approached with an invitation. "Hey, so we're all heading to Jake's family cabin this weekend for the Fourth. It's up by the falls, and it *literally* has the best view of the fireworks. You in?"

Zane was already fitting in. "Yeah, for sure. Sounds sick." His first summer in Paradise Falls was shaping up to be pretty awesome.

CHAPTER TWO

Zane, Star, and Dexter piled into Jake's pickup and headed to the cabin for the weekend. Each turn in the road revealed new mountains, lakes, and streams. Zane realized Paradise Falls was more than just concrete strip malls and parking lots. True to its name, the town really did have picture-perfect waterfalls.

Jake sat behind the wheel of his blue Ford F-250, blasting his new summer playlist—mostly pop-punk, with a few Top 40 hits mixed in. Dexter rode shotgun, bopping along to the music. Star and Zane sat in the truck bed, taking in the fresh summer air with Jake's playful beagle, Biscuits.

Zane admired the quaint scenery. He felt a tug at his heart. *There's magic here in Paradise Falls.*

They pulled up to Patriot Pete's Pit Stop, a gas station and general store with an American flag floating above it. Signs advertised fireworks and firecrackers. Dexter's eyes lit up with excitement.

Inside, the store was a mishmash of everything. They loaded a basket with burgers, hot dogs, buns, macaroni salad, and potato chips. For dessert, they grabbed a tub of frosted sugar cookies alongside marshmallows, chocolate bars, and graham crackers for s'mores.

Star and Zane struck playful poses, modeling sunglasses and hats for each other. Meanwhile, Jake attempted to use a questionable fake ID to buy a case of beer and a mason jar of watermelon moonshine. The cashier, a woman in her mid-fifties with a sharp eye, squinted at the ID. "Forty? Really?"

Jake thought fast and flashed his signature grin. "Well, you know, this mountain air keeps you lookin' young!"

Holding two boxes of firecrackers, Dexter leaned in with a conspiratorial whisper. "*Daddy,* can we get these?"

Jake played along, ruffling Dexter's hair affectionately. "Only if you promise not to blow up the garage again, *Son.*"

It was a painfully unconvincing act, but the cashier chuckled. "Alright, alright. Just don't let the sheriff catch you with that moonshine."

At the last minute, Dexter tossed a squeaky rubber cheeseburger into their basket. "Oh, and this," he said, wagging his eyebrows, "for Biscuits."

Jake shook his head. "You spoil my dog more than I do!"

With their supplies in tow, the group returned to the truck, excited and ready for a super fun weekend.

Jake's family cabin sat on a small lake. It had a wraparound porch that was tailor-made for drunken late nights filled with laughter. The charming house had wood-paneled walls and cozy couches with plenty of blankets and pillows. Antlers hung among wildlife paintings, paying homage to the world outside. A stone fireplace dominated the living room.

The friends unloaded the groceries and settled in.

"Come on, guys!" Jake said, already in his swim trunks. "Last one in the water's on dish duty tonight!" Without hesitation, he dashed toward the lake, tossing his phone to Dexter. "Record this!" Jake leaped onto a tire swing, whooped loudly, and flipped into the water, making a huge splash.

Biscuits zipped after Jake and dove in with a bark.

Star pulled Zane by the hand. "Race you!" Stripping as she went, she was down to her underwear by the time she reached the water and jumped in.

Excited, Zane pulled off his t-shirt and shorts and ran into the lake behind her. They splashed each other like children. Biscuits swam up to them, barking.

Zane and Star swam to a floating dock. Zane climbed up first, then extended a hand to help Star. Her fingers slipped into his, soft but strong.

"The sun feels good," Star said as she wrung out her hair, sending droplets down her shoulders. Zane's eyes followed the water's path, lingering longer than he intended.

"Yeah, it does," Zane agreed, laying back on the warm wooden planks, trying to appear casual.

"I love all your tattoos," Star said, admiring his inked body. Her fingers brushed his forearm, circling over a murky black shape.

He stiffened slightly.

"What's this one?"

"That was my first," he admitted. "Gave it to myself with a safety pin and a ballpoint pen. It's supposed to be a scorpion, 'cause I'm a Scorpio. Pretty stupid, right?"

Her touch didn't leave him. "I like it. It's mysterious, like you." She slid her finger over his wet chest, stopping at a small crescent mark.

Zane's breath caught as she tilted her head to meet his eyes.

"What about this one? Is it a moon?"

"Ha, that's actually just a birthmark. I've always had it."

"You're so cosmic," she whispered, her words curling around him like a spell.

"Hey!" Jake called out. "Where's Dex?"

As if on cue, Dexter burst out of the cabin with a ducky inflatable tube around his waist and a beer in each hand. He waded into the water with exaggerated caution, letting the tube lift under his arms to keep him afloat. "This is the life, ain't it?" he said, raising a beer to his lips.

The distant whistle of a train serenaded them from across the lake.

They drank, swam, and tubed around all afternoon. It was one of those perfect summer days that seemed to stretch on forever.

When hunger finally called, they moved to the porch. Jake grilled up the burgers and dogs as Star and Zane set the table with paper plates and their earlier haul from the pit stop.

Jake placed some burger patties on the table. "Honestly, this is better than any family trip I've ever had here. You guys are way more chill than my 12-year-old sister. All she does is talk, nonstop. And she never leaves me alone… with a million questions about every single thing I do."

"Aww," Star cooed. "She just loves her big bro."

Jake rolled his eyes. "Yeah, I love her to bits, too. But it's all, 'Where are you going? What are you doing? Who's that? Why aren't you answering me?' It's like she's majoring in nosiness with a minor in my life."

Star giggled. "Well, duh. As a former 12-year-old girl, I can confirm that it's literally our job to get all up in everyone's business."

Meanwhile, Dexter was constructing a sandwich that defied gravity—a burger, a hot dog, macaroni salad, and potato chips, all slathered in ketchup, mustard, and chipotle mayo. With a triumphant grin, he announced, "Behold, the Dex-Deluxe!"

Star gagged. "Ew, I'm not giving you mouth-to-mouth when that thing sends you into cardiac arrest."

Up to the challenge, Dexter took a monstrous bite of his messy creation. Unsurprisingly, most of the sandwich ended up falling to his feet.

Ever the opportunist, Biscuits scurried over, frantically engulfing everything in sight.

Dexter quipped, "Hot diggity dog, that pup's got taste!"

Biscuits barked in agreement, or perhaps he was asking for more. It was turning out to be the perfect summer day for everyone.

That evening, they journeyed up a mountain road to a lookout point. The twinkling lights of Paradise Falls spread out below them. They parked at the summit and clambered onto the truck bed, the jar of moonshine making its rounds.

Above them, the sky erupted in vibrant colors as the city's fireworks display began. Star was right—this had to be the best view in town. Jake clapped, and Dexter ooh-ed and aah-ed.

But not everyone was a fan of the loud booms. Biscuits, the bewildered beagle, whimpered and burrowed himself behind Zane.

As a particularly bright firework lit up the sky, Zane's eyes found Star. With her two long braids, oversized flannel shirt, and cutoff jean shorts, she looked every bit the picture of summer perfection. She was beautiful.

Jake jumped up when the show ended. "Man, those were epic!" He looked at Dexter and pulled out his phone. "But I bet we can do better! Ready to make some content?"

Dexter waved the firecrackers they had purchased earlier. "Hell yeah!"

Jake pumped his fist in the air. "Let's goooo!" And with that declaration, the two mischief-makers bounded off, leaving Star, Zane, and the still-anxious Biscuits behind.

Crickets chirped and a distant frog croaked. Leaves rustled as the wind swept through the trees. And somewhere in the distance, the unmistakable pops and crackles of firecrackers were punctuated by the delighted hollers of Jake and Dexter.

Star toyed with one of her braids. "Alright, mystery man," she said, poking at Zane's thigh. "You're always so quiet. What's your origin story? Where'd you roll in from?" She followed the question with a playful purse of her lips, and Zane saw the faint outline of a heart in their shape.

Zane ruffled his short hair. "Well, not much to tell. I lost my parents when I was young and don't really remember them. Grew up bouncing from one house to another," he admitted, his casual tone masking the underlying complexity of his situation. He was feeling drunk and more willing to open up. He pulled out a worn leather wallet from his back pocket and extracted a single, faded photograph from its folds.

Star watched him curiously. "Is that...?"

"The only picture I have of 'em," Zane explained, offering her a small, nostalgic smile. He handed the picture over to her gently, like a sacred relic.

Star studied the image in the moonlight. "Your dad... You look just like him, Zane." It was true. The resemblance was undeniable. "That's rough. I'm sorry you never got to know them."

Zane took the picture back and tucked it into his wallet. "I'm fine on my own. When you've moved as much as I have, you learn to take care of yourself."

"Seems lonely." Star's eyes softened. "So, did you ever have *any* friends?"

"Yeah, a few—mostly dudes from the skate park. Nothing heavy. We'd just mess around, hit some tricks, drink, smoke, vibe..."

"What about *girlfriends*?"

"Haha, yeah, I get around," Zane hyped himself up, though he immediately felt self-conscious. "Never anything serious, though." It was true, he'd had sex a few times with a few girls, but it was always a bit awkward and never led to anything real. It was fun, sure, but there was never that spark to make it more.

"Interesting." Star tilted her head, intrigued. "So, if a girl didn't bring you here, what did? How'd you end up in Paradise Falls?"

"Ah, well, that's another story. I inherited a house from a great-uncle I never knew. Wild, huh?"

"Stop it, you're kidding!" She slapped his knee and inched closer to him. "Seriously?"

"Yup, no lie. There was no one else left, so I got everything."

"Oh my God, how did he die?"

Zane responded, "He was just really old, I guess. I dunno. I never met him. I just found out he existed after he died."

She leaned in, mock suspicion in her eyes. "Your origin story is like something out of a Marvel movie. What else are you hiding? Any *superhero* secrets you're keeping from me?"

He laughed, "Only if you count mastering the art of microwaving ramen noodles."

"Pity. You could totally rock the spandex," she teased, then licked her lips.

"Yeah, uh… Spandex isn't really my thing." Zane felt objectified, but he kind of liked it. He'd already been practically naked in front of Star earlier at the lake, dripping wet in his underwear. But now, he felt even more exposed — the thought of her picturing him in tights made his blood pump harder. He shifted in his seat. "So, what about you? You sure ask a lot of questions. Are you, like, some kind of undercover FBI interrogator?"

"Something like that." Star flipped her hair with a coy

wink. "Actually, my life is pretty dull compared to yours. I've been here in Paradise Falls my whole life. My parents travel, like, nonstop. My grandma, Grammy, practically raised me. She lives with me, but she's like a million years old and doesn't do much."

"So, you basically live alone, too?"

"Yeah, basically. I kind of get how it feels not to have a close family. That's why I work at Snaxtime. I get out of the house, make some cash, and meet new people — like you."

"It kinda feels like we were supposed to meet… You and me."

"I totally feel that, too."

The space between them shrunk. Their eyes locked and their faces inched closer. Just as their lips were about to meet...

Jake and Dexter burst out of the woods, sprinting toward the truck and laughing wildly. Zane and Star both jerked back, the spell between them broken.

Jake, catching his breath, shouted, "Y'all ready to roll? We're fresh out of firecrackers and moonshine!"

Dexter fumbled a bit as he hopped into the truck. "Those s'mores ain't gonna make themselves!"

Star let out a small, nervous laugh, brushing a stray hair behind her ear as if nothing had happened. "Guess we'll have to save that for later," she whispered in Zane's ear.

Zane acted cool, but his mind was stuck on what had almost happened, wondering if "later" would ever come.

When they returned to the cabin, the group gathered around the fire pit to toast marshmallows and finish off the beer. Zane glanced over at Star. The gentle glow from the fire highlighted the curves of her face, and Zane felt a warmth that had nothing to do with the flames.

He thought to himself how incredibly fortunate he was to be there. He took his charred marshmallow out of the fire, added it to a graham cracker with chocolate, and then took a bite of the s'more. It was sweet and delicious — the perfect end to a perfect day. He wished with all his heart that the rest of the summer would be just as special.

CHAPTER THREE

Within a few weeks, Zane had become a pro. He could do it all: grill, flip, fry, and ring up orders. He fit right in. He'd gotten to know — and like — the entire Snaxtime staff. But Star, Dexter, and Jake were more than colleagues; they'd gotten really tight.

It was just a regular Wednesday night, and the gang was wrapping up their shifts. Jake had the day off, and Marjorie was tucked away in her office, doing whatever managers do.

Dexter was wiping down the coffee station when a pot of decaf slid off the counter and shattered on the floor. Coffee splattered everywhere.

"Ay, caramba!" he exclaimed.

"Yikes, need a hand with that, Dex?" Zane offered.

"Nah, I got this." Dexter sighed. "Actually, could ya snag me a box of coffee filters from the basement?"

"Sure thing." Zane went down the stairs and flipped on the lights. Shelves were cluttered with supplies. "Where are you, filters?"

But as soon as he stepped into the room, something felt off. It was like the walls were closing in on him, warping and shifting. A wave of dizziness hit him hard, and his arms and legs felt heavy like they were made of lead.

He spotted a metal cabinet against the back wall. It called to him. Even though he felt weak and nauseous, he had to know what was inside.

Static buzzed in his ears. Through the white noise, he heard a raspy, steady, rhythmic sound—like someone breathing.

The lights went out.

In the dark, Zane found the cabinet. It opened with a click. He reached inside and closed his fingers around a hard, thick object. He grabbed it and turned back to the exit.

Zane scrambled up the stairs on shaky legs. Emerging into the light, he gulped for fresh air.

Everything was hazy. *What just happened?*

Zane found Star reading a paperback in the break room. When he saw her, he almost completely forgot about the basement. She was so pretty.

"Hey," Zane said trying to sound casual. "What're you reading?"

Star looked up from her book and smiled. "It's a biography on Tammy Faye Bakker."

"Who?"

"Um, only the most boss bitch ever! She was this sassy televangelist lady who built a massive TV ministry with her husband. When he got caught up in scandal and went to prison, she didn't let that stop her. She was, like, super resilient and stayed totally dedicated to her calling, all while serving killer eyeliner and lashes for days. Iconic."

"Oh whoa, never heard of her. That's cool. I didn't realize you were into the whole Jesus thing."

"Like, definitely not. But I still think there's something really powerful about sticking to your faith, even when the world's against you." She closed her book. "So, what're *you* reading?"

"Huh?"

"That big book you're holding."

Zane looked down, puzzled. He was indeed holding a book. It was old and bound in leather. "I don't know. I was heading into the basement and got lightheaded and... Next thing I know... I was back here with you."

Dexter burst in. "Hey Zane, got those filters?"

Zane frowned at the book. "Uh, no. I guess I found this instead. Totally blanked. This is so weird. I could've sworn I got the filters. Actually, I don't even remember going down into the basement at all."

"Whoa, what is it?" Dexter took the book from Zane and read the inside cover. *"Property of Harold Snaxton."*

Star's eyes popped. "Shut up! Let me see that!" She snatched the book from Dexter's hands. "Harold Snaxton founded Snaxtime. He's practically a legend!"

"What's inside? His original recipes?" Dexter was getting excited—he fancied himself a top chef, especially when it came to fried food.

She flipped through the pages. "Oh my God, it totally *does* have a bunch of recipes. We're going to have a blast with this. We have to make one!"

Zane looked over her shoulder. "It's not just recipes. Look at these drawings and all these handwritten notes everywhere. Is that... poetry?"

Dexter pointed at a diagram of a hot dog being injected with cheese. "Ah, look! The birth of the first cheese dog, the missing *link* in gastronomic evolution!"

Engrossed, Star turned the page. "Yeah, this is way more than a cookbook." She couldn't believe what she was reading. "It's a window into one of America's greatest minds. Harold Snaxton basically invented fast food."

She landed on a page titled *Snaxton's Special Sauce.* The recipe promised to be both irresistible and addictive.

"Let's go with this one," Star exclaimed. "It has some weird directions, but it looks easy enough, and we can make it now before we close. I mean, why not?"

The trio plunged headfirst into their spontaneous culinary adventure. Like treasure hunters, they unearthed every obscure item required from the well-stocked kitchen. The mysterious recipe listed over 20 ingredients: common staples like ketchup, mayo, and mustard; more exotic flavors like smoked paprika and soy sauce; and oddballs—a dash of pickle juice, a spoonful of grape jelly, even a few splashes of root beer.

One by one, they measured each ingredient and added them to the pan. It started to simmer.

They put in the prescribed amount of pickle juice and jelly. The root beer fizzed and popped as they poured it. It smelled sweet and earthy.

Following the instructions, Star stirred the sauce with a large wooden spoon exactly thirteen times. The bubbles grew lazier as the sauce thickened and transformed into a rich, velvety concoction.

Star pointed at the recipe. "It's telling us to say these strange words."

"Like a spell?" Dexter asked.

She shrugged. "I mean, whatever, we've gotten this far."

Together they read aloud off the page, "*Vexna pyrone zendu.*"

The sauce boiled furiously for several seconds before flashing with a burst of fiery sparks. It settled just as quickly.

"Uh, was that supposed to happen?" Zane asked.

"Your guess is as good as mine. Ready to taste it?" Star asked, holding out a spoonful in her hand.

Zane hesitated. "What do we dip in it?"

"Give me a sec," Dexter said, already firing up the deep fryer. He dunked a basket of tater tots into the hot oil. In just a few minutes, they were ready.

Without missing a beat, Dexter grabbed a hot tot and generously swirled it in the pearly pink sauce before tossing it into his mouth.

His eyes bulged open in astonishment, and he squealed with approval. "WHOA!!" He seized another handful of tots, plunging them one by one into the sauce and then into his mouth. "You have to try this," he insisted.

Star and Zane took apprehensive nibbles. The taste that greeted them was unlike anything they had ever experienced. A perfect blend of sweet, tangy, and savory, the sauce twirled across their palates in a tantalizing tango. And once the dance began, they couldn't stop. Each bite amplified their desire for more. They devoured the tots as if under a spell.

With their fingers dripping in sauce, they had let all manners fall to the wayside. They slurped and licked the remnants off their digits like famished beasts.

With no more taters in sight, they cooked up more items to pair with the sauce. They drizzled it over crispy chicken nuggets, a fried fish sandwich, and a cheese dog. They even bravely dunked a glazed donut into it. Under the influence of the elixir, the sweet pastry blossomed with brilliant new flavors.

"Is there anything this sauce *doesn't* make better?" Zane marveled, polishing off his donut.

"It's like a magic potion that makes everything taste like heaven." Star dipped her finger into the pan and brought it to her awaiting mouth, sucking the sauce with pleasure.

Even with full bellies, they couldn't resist. The sauce was indeed something special.

"Oh my God," Star erupted in ecstasy. "We have to get Marjorie to add this to the menu. People would literally die."

Dexter was on board immediately. "Marjorie's still in her office, I think," he affirmed, pushing back his chair to stand. "Let's go pitch this."

Their sneakers squeaked against the linoleum floor as they scurried out of the kitchen and over to Marjorie's office. Dexter rapped on the door until she called out.

"Come in!" came Marjorie's voice from the other side. As they filed into her office, they were met with the soft tapping of Marjorie's fingers on her keyboard.

Dexter cleared his throat, "Marjorie, we have an idea we want to discuss with you."

Marjorie swiveled and leaned back in her chair. "Go ahead, Mr. Hernandez. I'm listening."

Dexter began, "Well, we found a bunch of these OG Snaxtime recipes..."

"And," Star chimed in, her hands clasping the journal as if it were a priceless artifact, "We made one... Harold Snaxton's Special Sauce. It's... You just have to taste it. It's literally addictive."

"This sauce could be a total game-changer. We think maybe it should be on the menu, like as a limited-edition item," Zane said.

Marjorie had reservations. To her, the establishment operated with the precision of clockwork, every part ticking in perfect sync. The introduction of an impromptu, off-menu item was, in her perspective, tossing a wrench into the gears. Also, these kids looked high as hell.

"Absolutely not," she asserted, her arms folding across her chest as if to create a physical barrier to the proposal. "This is a franchise establishment, not some experimental test kitchen." Her austere gaze swept over the eager faces before her, a silent yet potent declaration that the debate was closed.

But her trio of innovators wasn't quite ready to throw in the towel.

"But Marjorie," Star begged, "this isn't just any sauce. It's from Harold Snaxton himself—a Snaxtime original recipe."

"Yeah, and we're *lovin' it!*" Dexter added with both thumbs up.

Zane pleaded, "C'mon Marjorie, at least taste it. We wouldn't bug you if it wasn't totally insane."

"*Insane* isn't exactly what we're going for here at Snaxtime. And I can't just make alterations to the menu on a whim," Marjorie responded. "But color me curious... Let me give this magic sauce a taste."

Dexter darted out of the room. He was back in no time with a basket of hot, crispy Cheesy Stix, generously slathered with their newly crafted sauce. He set it down in front of a skeptical Marjorie.

"This better be good." Marjorie picked up a stick and eyed it before taking a tentative bite. Her reluctance was replaced by delight, then shock.

She reached out for another cheese stick, then another. The taste was too compelling, too enticing to resist. The sauce was a triumph, an absolute sensation, and Marjorie had no choice but to concede.

"Fine," she sighed, wiping a glob of sauce from her lips and licking it off her finger. "We'll trial run it during tomorrow's lunch shift. But first things first, put that in a bottle. I'm taking some home!"

That night, the special sauce haunted their dreams.

Star dreamt that the sauce was the key ingredient in a new luxury line of beauty products. She bathed in it, smothering her skin in the thick pink sauce. She washed her hair in it, its sweet perfume flooding her senses as she lathered it through her locks. She applied lipstick made with the sauce. The taste was irresistible. She kept putting it on until it was down to a nub. She couldn't stop licking and biting her lips to get more flavor. When Star woke up, her lips were raw and sore.

Dexter was lost in a fantastical landscape where sauce streams flowed amidst a backdrop of giant dancing French fries and hamburger hills. He plunged into a river of sauce, gulping down mouthfuls of the glorious liquid. He swam deeper, drowning in the intense taste. He awoke gasping for air.

Zane dreamed of a fountain gushing with creamy sauce. But tragically, he was a captive, chained just out of reach. This proximity turned torturous as he was unable to indulge in its copious flows. Desperate, he stretched out his tongue, trying to catch even a drop. He awoke with a dry mouth, his longing for the sauce still unfulfilled.

Even Marjorie was trapped in a bizarre dream. She was a contestant on a twisted version of *Iron Chef*, where Snaxton's Special Sauce was the featured ingredient. But as the competition heated up, the nightmare took a darker turn: Marjorie became part of the dish, helplessly simmering in a vat of the sauce as giant talking hot dog judges circled, critiquing her flavor. She woke up in a puddle of sweat.

The fever dreams resulted in a brutal morning; they were exhausted, weak, and in agony as if nursing the world's worst hangover. Nonetheless, they pushed forward as they prepared for work. More than anything, they were craving more sauce.

Marjorie was waiting at the front door when Zane, Star, and Dexter arrived at Snaxtime right before dawn.

"You're late!" she barked. Her tone was sharp and impatient, unlike her usual cheerful self.

None of them felt quite like themselves. Irritability afflicted them all.

"Let's get to work, chop chop!" Marjorie clapped, the harsh sound making them flinch. "We've got sauce to make."

They shuffled inside without protest and got to work. Unlike their previous sauce-making session, this one felt strained and frazzled. Marjorie watched over them like a drill sergeant.

By the time Jake arrived, he found them in the throes of a sauce-making frenzy, looking like they'd battled insomnia all night. "Um, did I miss the party last night? Y'all look like hell and you're actin' sus."

"Ew, nobody asked for your dumb opinions, Jake," Star snapped.

They all glared at him.

He held up his hands in defense. "Whoa, good morning to you too!"

Marjorie followed up with a ferocious attack. "I'd call you a piece of trash, but that would be an insult to garbage!"

Jake gasped.

"*Oh my!*" Marjorie threw her hands onto her chest in a moment of clarity. "I'm so sorry, Jake, I don't know what just came over me."

Jake's confusion was clear. "What's goin' on here? I take one day off, and y'all get body snatched or somethin'?"

As the aroma drifted up from the simmering concoction, an intoxicating spell was cast upon them. Star, Dexter, Zane, and Marjorie crowded around the stove like zombies, their mouths drooling. Again, they recited the words from the book, "*Vexna pyrone zendu.*" It sparked and bubbled.

Jake jumped back. "What the hell?!"

But they remained transfixed. The world faded away until it was just them and the pot of temptation.

Dexter dipped his finger in for a taste, the flavor flooding his senses with euphoria. "It's ready!"

Jake looked on in disbelief. "Dude, you just stuck your finger in there! That's *definitely* a health code violation."

They all ignored him and dove in like starved animals.

"Um, guys?"

Star lunged at him, cramming a sauce-covered tater tot into his mouth. One taste was all it took — Jake's confusion crumbled and his eyes glassed over. He was hooked.

"How can I help?"

"Get on that phone of yours and tell the world!" Marjorie instructed.

Jake, who had a massive social media following, filmed himself shirtless for the cause, knowing it would generate more interest. He dunked a Jalapeño Hot Bite into the sauce and provocatively shoved it into his mouth, allowing some of it to drip onto his chest.

"DAY-UM," he proclaimed while wiping the sauce off his body and bringing it up to his lips. "We just discovered the ORIGINAL recipe for this WILD sauce here at Snaxtime, and it's FIRE." He ate another popper. "Seriously, I can't stop. You GOTTA try it. Come by and sample it, today only, here at the one-and-only OG Snaxtime in Paradise Falls!"

Jake was rambling on, talking fast, manic, high on the sauce. His eyes were completely dilated and bugged out like he was on something stronger than just a condiment. But his fans probably wouldn't even notice; they'd be too focused on his abs.

His post went viral within a blink.

Marjorie initiated the rest of the morning staff as they arrived, giving them all a taste and instructions for the new product launch. Sure enough, everyone was on board.

And so, the Limited Edition Snaxton's Special Sauce was proudly unveiled, billed as the original secret recipe of Snaxtime's legendary founder.

A small crowd gathered as patrons jockeyed for position to get a sauce sample. Excited murmurs rippled through the line.

The crew watched in delight as each customer took their first taste. Eyes would widen, faces flush, and moans of bliss would sound.

It didn't take long before the line wrapped around the building and spilled into the parking lot. Customers were licking their cups clean and then getting back in line for more.

The flavor enraptured kids and adults alike, the hypnotic palette of sweet, tangy, and savory dazzled their taste buds. The reviews were unanimous:

"I've never tasted anything like it!"

"Lord almighty, this sauce is heaven!"

"This stuff should be illegal!"

"I need a gallon of this, stat!"

"I'd sell my soul for this sauce!"

"Gimme more!"

The crew had struck gold, and word spread quickly. The sauce's sparkle attracted masses from near and far, all eager to experience the wonder of Snaxton's secret recipe. For now, it was the undisputed star of Paradise Falls.

However, the initial joy of their success devolved into something less cheerful. It soon turned into hysteria. The kitchen was under siege, buried beneath an avalanche of demand.

Ingredients were hastily combined to keep up. They labored tirelessly, but their efforts were swallowed up by the monstrous appetite of the masses, who kept coming back for more. The once plentiful ingredients vanished at an alarming rate.

"We need more sauce up here!" Marjorie called out from

the front.

"Oh no," Dexter groaned.

Caught in the whirlwind of frying and saucing, Zane turned to him sharply. "Oh no, what?"

Dexter held up an empty jar of grape jelly. The inevitable had finally struck. A critical ingredient was gone.

Star proposed a workaround. "Just use strawberry. We have plenty of that."

Desperate to keep the situation under control, they substituted grape jelly with strawberry. The taste was close to the original, almost indistinguishable.

But instead of placating the sauce-hungry crowd, the altered recipe only fanned the flames of frustration. It lacked the same potent magical effect. A rumble of discontent rolled through the restaurant.

A man approached the counter with his tray of food. His face was contorted with anger. "What's *this*? This isn't the same sauce! It's SHIT!"

Marjorie tried to reason with the furious customer. "Sir, we are sorry for the inconvenience, but…"

The man flung his tray at Marjorie. The crowd gasped as food and sauce splattered across her entire body and face.

A full-blown food fight erupted. Customers began hurling their meals and the fake sauce at each other, turning the restaurant into complete chaos.

"That's it, everyone OUT!" Marjorie screamed while pulling the fire alarm. "Snaxtime is CLOSED!"

Customers were forced out of the dining room, and Jake locked the doors behind them. Still, the crowd continued to scream and bang on the glass from outside.

Food was everywhere.

"Um, that was a little too extra," Star conceded.

Dexter collapsed into a booth. "I don't think the strawberry jelly was a hit."

Jake looked at his phone, his face growing paler with every swipe. Negative comments were flooding in, and his follower count was plummeting. "Oh, hell no!"

"What's up, dude?" Zane asked, noticing the panic in Jake's eyes.

"That sauce screwed me! I just lost ten thousand followers! I'm never gonna recover from this. Don't EVER mention that stupid recipe book again!" Jake yanked off his hat and stormed into the back, fuming.

"Exactly why I said stick to the menu. Remember this next time you want to experiment. Now, put that silly book back where you found it." Marjorie picked a pickle slice out of her hair. "Let's get this place back to normal."

Despite the sauce fiasco and Jake and Marjorie's rejection of the book, Zane, Star, and Dexter were still eager to dive deeper into the journal. They read it in secret whenever they could. Within its pages, Harold Snaxton emerged as a mysterious character. The Snaxtime icon was revealed as a figure with many layers.

Snaxton had a penchant for the strange and unusual. More than mere recipes, the book brimmed with tales of peculiar rituals and practices bordering on the occult.

The pages within the journal were a fusion of science, magic, and gastronomy. There were star charts and lunar calendars connected to different recipes, like *Moonlight Meatloaf* and *Cosmic Chicken Casserole*. There were diagrams of early alchemical soda machines and deep fryers. There was a recipe for a love potion milkshake that called for rose water and a can of sardines. There was even a sacrificial ritual for weight loss that called for a pig's snout.

It all painted a picture of a man who embraced the unknown. For Harold, the supernatural was the secret spice in his larger recipe for success.

One evening after hours, Zane, Star, and Dexter gathered in the restaurant's basement. Boxes of supplies, plastic cups, and jumbo-sized cans of ketchup, pickles, and cheese sauce were stacked to the ceiling. A vent blew cool air into the room. This was the stage for the trio's next exploration into Harold Snaxton's world. They clustered around the journal.

Dexter's glasses teetered on the edge of his nose. "Look, a recipe for a 'Midnight Tart.'" He grinned at Star. "Hey, isn't that what they call you after three margaritas?"

She elbowed him in the ribs. "You're pushing it, buddy. *Everyone* knows I'm a vodka girl."

As they dove further into the journal, Zane mused aloud, "You guys ever think Harold's magical food experiments might be why Snaxtime is such a hit?"

Dexter pondered, "Yeah, totally. That sauce wasn't just super — it was *supernatural*."

Star added, "That would explain my total obsession with their Chicken Nibbles and honey mustard." She flipped through a few pages. "Guys, this journal isn't just about making addicting food. It's about harnessing real magic. Think about it — what if we tried something else from this book?"

"Like what?" Dexter asked.

Star pointed at an intricate design. "BINGO, this one," she said, tracing her finger over the words to an incantation. "It looks like it's supposed to be some kind of cleansing ritual. I still have a killer hangover from all the sauce drama the other day. Snaxtime could totally use, like, a serious energy makeover right now."

Dexter squinted at the page. "You sure about this, Star? I can't handle another sauce-pocalypse."

"Okay, the sauce thing did get a *little* messy, but this isn't even a recipe. It looks super simple. We just light a candle and say a few words. I mean, what could *actually* go wrong? We conjure up the Stay Puft Marshmallow Man?"

Dexter shrugged. "I do love marshmallows. Sure, why not?"

Star turned to face Zane. "You've been quiet. Ready to

join our coven?"

Zane was visibly wrestling with the proposition. Something was wrong. "Maybe Jake was right about not wanting anything to do with this book. That whole sauce thing was completely outta control. Maybe I'll sit this one out."

Star's expression shifted. "Seriously? Just when I thought you were adventurous."

"I… I'm just not feelin' it. Sorry." Zane was acutely aware of his friends' letdown, but something within him was raising alarm bells.

"Are you for real right now?" Star sidled up to him, clasping his hands in hers. She used her most persuasive voice and batted her long lashes to coax him. "It would mean the world to me if you joined us."

Zane couldn't help but smile at her charm offensive. "Alright, fine."

With consensus reached, Star clapped her hands excitedly. They prepared for the ritual. Following the instructions, they poured a circle of salt on the floor. The granules crunched under their shoes.

They turned off the lights. In the center of their circle, they placed the open book and lit a single candle.

They joined hands and began the incantation. The words were written in an elegant, flowing script. It was a language they didn't recognize, the syllables foreign and strange on their tongues. "*Zu-vin solas... Zu-vin solas...*" The alien syllables filled the cold room.

♦

Deep underground, a tomb untouched by daylight shivered.

♦

As the trio continued, their recitation gained strength. "*Zu-vin solas... Zu-vin solas...*" The chant unfolded in an instinctive rhythm.

♦

Inside a bejeweled sarcophagus, something responded to their summons. A faint gasp cut through the stagnant air. Its ancient occupant, roused from a deep and lengthy slumber, began to stir.

♦

An intense bolt of energy shot through Zane. Startled, he let go of his friends' hands.

The candle snuffed out, plunging them into darkness. Silence filled the room, broken only by their shaky breaths. It seemed their ritual had failed.

"What was that, Zane?! Why did you let go?" Star's voice pierced the darkness, irritation coloring her words as she flicked on her phone's flashlight.

Zane was still recovering. "Didn't you guys feel that? There was this... shock... It went through me."

Star and Dexter both shook their heads. Zane just shrugged. He knew he'd messed up, but he'd never felt anything like that before.

Disappointed, they cleaned up the evidence of their botched experiment and returned upstairs to finish closing for the night.

Little Donna-Jo hated going to church every Sunday with her family, but she knew it meant going to Snaxtime afterward. The promise of a Kid's Time Meal, especially the hamburger, her absolute favorite, and the much-anticipated toy, made the Sunday routine bearable.

Today was no different. She had patiently made it through another service in another itchy dress, and now it was time to feast. She couldn't wait to see what was inside as she opened her meal box.

Donna-Jo had her heart set on Donut Kitty, the final plushy toy needed to complete her collection. But when she reached into the box, she pulled out a measly three-pack of crayons instead. Disappointed but hungry, she bit into a tater tot. It was cold and mushy.

She went for the burger. She unwrapped it and took an eager, big bite. But the taste was disgusting, and her nose wrinkled at a yucky smell. She looked down at the sandwich in her hands. The sight was horrifying—the meat was greenish-gray and crawling with thick, juicy maggots! She spat it out, screamed, and burst into tears.

Chaos erupted as more customers discovered rotten

meat in their meals. Some people bolted for the bathrooms, clutching their stomachs, while others vomited right there in the dining room. A furious mob gathered at the counter, shouting in disgust.

Marjorie yelled out to the kitchen, "What the hell is going on with the meat?!"

Chucky, a pimply teen, poked his head out from behind the grill. "I don't know, ma'am… I swear it looked fine!"

"Well, somethin's not right! Go check the fridge!"

Chucky scrambled to the back to investigate. The refrigerator was running fine, and the meat wasn't expired, but the stench of rot hit him hard. Maggots were squirming everywhere. The poor teen took one look, his eyes rolled back, and he dropped like a sack of potatoes.

It defied logic—like they were the victims of a sick prank. The staff worked quickly to discard the spoiled food and clean the fridge.

A disaster like this could lead to a permanent shutdown and ruin Snaxtime's reputation for good. Marjorie scrambled to calm the angry patrons, offering apologies, refunds, and gift cards.

Once again, they closed the restaurant for the day.

Snaxtime remained under a cloud of misfortune in the days following the unsettling incident. Marjorie had her hands full with a string of other anomalies.

One late afternoon, she and Star were doing inventory when Star paused on a row of boxes filled with sugar packets. "Ew, gross, look at this!"

Marjorie walked over. The edges of the cardboard were gnawed away, and ripped-up packets of sugar were everywhere. "What in the world..."

"Something's been eating all the sugar," Star said.

Marjorie picked up one of the boxes and examined it closely. "Looks like we got rats again."

They spent the next hour inspecting every corner of the storage area, finding more signs of the mysterious visitor. Bite marks on food packages and scattered crumbs told a story of an uninvited guest making itself at home.

Marjorie sighed and put her hands on her hips. "We can't afford any more problems after the other day. I'll call the exterminator first thing tomorrow."

It was late one night, and the restaurant was empty. Latoya, a sweet older woman who'd been working at Snaxtime longer than anyone could remember, sang to herself as she wiped down the milkshake machine.

Suddenly, the blender went berserk. Latoya's silver cross necklace snagged in the spinning metal blades, yanking her toward the grinding machinery.

"HELP!" Latoya choked out as the chain tightened around her neck.

Jake and Dexter bolted over. The machine pulled harder, the chain digging into her throat. Jake grabbed a knife from the counter and cut her free. Latoya fell back, clutching her neck as she slammed into the wall.

"Oh my God, are you okay?" Jake asked, hugging her.

She nodded, but she was shaken.

Dexter pulled the plug, but the motor didn't stop. The mixer spewed pink sludge like a geyser.

Then the entire kitchen went haywire. The dishwasher rattled, the deep fryers hissed and bubbled, and the soda fountain shot streams across the room.

"Nope, nope, nope," Dexter muttered, panicking.

"Lord Jesus!" Latoya exclaimed as the boys huddled around her.

The lights strobed, the machines beeped, buzzed, and clanged. The whole kitchen felt like it was about to explode.

Just as quickly as it started, everything went silent. The lights steadied, and the machines powered down.

Jake wiped a hand across his face. "This place is cursed. Let's get the hell out of here."

Perhaps not wanting to be left out, the plumbing decided to join the series of unfortunate events. Toilets backed up one after another, flooding the restrooms and putting them out of order.

"Zane, get the plunger and sort out these toilets, would ya'?" Marjorie asked, shaking her head in defeat. "See if you can get things flowing again."

Zane sighed, grabbing a heavy-duty plunger and mop from the supply closet. Cleaning up other people's crap wasn't part of his regular duties, but with staff quitting left and right, they'd all been taking turns.

He started in the men's room, a cramped space tiled in mint green. He plunged the grimy toilet in the single stall. After a few labored pumps, it gurgled and the disgusting mess disappeared with a satisfying swoosh. He gave it an extra flush for good measure, then moved to the sink to wash his hands.

The pink soap dispenser wheezed out a glop of floral foam. Zane worked up a bubbly lather and rinsed his hands under the sharp spray of the sink.

Suddenly, the lights went out.

"Very funny, Dexter!" Zane yelled. But no response came. This wasn't Dexter's style.

Zane looked up to the mirror. In the pitch-black darkness, a pair of glowing ice-blue eyes materialized, floating and disembodied.

Zane's mouth dropped open to scream, but nothing came out.

The lights flickered back on. Zane blinked hard. His heart was pounding. The ghostly orbs were gone, leaving only his own wide-eyed, startled reflection staring back at him.

Speculation ran rampant, and half-joking remarks about a "Snaxtime curse" became a common theme. As days passed and bad things kept happening, the trio couldn't shake the nagging question—had their basement experiment unleashed something they didn't understand?

The inevitability of revisiting the ritual hung in the air.

It was a Friday night, and Star, Dexter, and Zane were alone after finishing their closing duties.

"Like, seriously, you guys," Star began, "I really think that redoing the ritual..." She glanced at Zane. "You know, the one *you* kinda messed up before, might totally reset everything."

"Nope. No way, José," Dexter protested. "Last time we did that, we basically entered *The Conjuring* universe."

"Look, I've spent hours studying this," Star said, gripping the journal. "And I'm, like, pretty sure if we just follow the instructions *exactly* and don't break the circle this time," she shot a pointed look at Zane, "everything will go back to normal."

"Things *did* start getting weird after I backed out last time." Zane sighed. "I guess... I don't see any other options. Let's try it again."

Outnumbered, Dexter threw up his hands in resignation. "Alright, so, when are we doing this?"

Star shrugged. "Well, I don't have anywhere to be right now, do you?"

They went back down to the basement and prepared for their repeat performance. Seated within the circle of salt and the journal open before them, they began the ritual again. This time, Zane wouldn't let his fear mess things up.

"*Zu-vin solas... Zu-vin solas...*"

As the chant spilled from their lips, a curious change swept the basement. The dusty air grew dense and cold. Their breaths came out in visible icy puffs. Zane swore the concrete floor was rippling beneath them.

Halfway through the incantation, the same intense jolt of energy shot through Zane's body. His muscles tensed up against the surge. He gritted his teeth, determined not to break the circle again. He wasn't going to let his friends down.

"*Zu-vin solas... Zu-vin solas...*"

Their voices rose in unison, the words of the chant intensifying. With a final, desperate shout, they completed the incantation.

The room fell still.

They held their breath, waiting for any sign that their ritual had worked.

And then they heard it.

"You have summoned me. I rise again."

CHAPTER FOUR

Paradise Falls, an aptly named slice of heaven or hell, depending on who you asked, was home to a gentlemen's club called "Kitten Heels." Located in the neon-lit heart of downtown, it hid behind blacked-out windows and a plain exterior. For the desperate, this was the place to be.

Inside, girls slinked around poles under pink and blue lights, their shadows shimmying on the grimy carpet. The air reeked of sweat, cheap booze, and bad decisions.

Ronny's mid-life crisis had dragged on far too long. Another typical night found him slumped over the bar, eyes glassy from one too many whiskeys. His gut spilled out of his half-tucked shirt. Crooked glasses and a scruffy mustache completed the look.

With an empty glass in hand, he got lost in an '80s rock song. He recognized the tune, but the name escaped him.

His phone buzzed—a text from his wife asking the usual question. He ignored it and waved at the bartender instead.

"Another double," Ronny slurred.

The bartender was an older woman with a bleached beehive, purple eyeshadow, and painted-on eyebrows. "This is your last round," she said in a raspy voice as she poured him a whiskey. "You've had enough for tonight, Ronny."

"The party's just gettin' started, Marlene," Ronny drawled, his attention diverted by the sight of a curvy cocktail waitress with bouncy black curls. Her red high heels left small dents in the carpet as she sashayed by.

"When you gettin' off work, baby?" Ronny patted her behind.

"In your dreams, creep." Her response was cutting. The two women shared a knowing look that left Ronny feeling decidedly less smug.

Ronny turned back to the bartender. "She's not my type anyway. I like 'em blonde," he declared, puckering his lips in an exaggerated kiss toward Marlene.

She shook her head, "You're a real charmer, Ronny." She wandered off to the other end of the bar to help other customers.

"Well, I need a smoke," Ronny declared, even though nobody was listening. Getting up from his bar stool was a challenge. His legs, wobbly from the onslaught of alcohol, almost gave out. With a grunt, he managed to stay upright and stumbled toward the back exit.

The alley behind Kitten Heels was narrow and littered with garbage and graffiti. The sounds of sirens and cars drifted in from afar. Steam hissed from a manhole. A green light above it made the escaping smoke look like toxic gas.

Ronny fumbled with his pack of cigarettes before pulling one out. He put it between his lips and searched his pockets for a lighter.

Suddenly, a beautiful, melodic hum caught his ear. Ronny froze, mesmerized by the tune.

From the steam, a stunning woman emerged. She had on a tight black leather dress and fishnet stockings. Her long hair was silky and black.

The cigarette fell from Ronny's open mouth to the ground. He bent to pick it up. When he lifted his head, the woman was somehow standing right in front of him. She stared him down with piercing blue eyes.

He stood slowly, his eyes never leaving hers as he came face to face with the mysterious woman. He gulped. "Got a light?"

She flicked her finger, and a flame sparked from her red nail, lighting Ronny's cigarette.

"Wow," he exclaimed. "What's a girl like you doing in a place like this? Please tell me you're dancing tonight." He took a long drag.

Before he could exhale, she reached out and grasped his shirt. She jerked him toward her and passionately sucked the smoke from his mouth, never breaking eye contact. The woman exhaled it back into his face and smiled. Her grin widened, revealing rows of pointed teeth.

A nearby police siren drowned out Ronny's screams as she tore into him. The lit cigarette fell from his fingers as his body jerked violently in her grip. The grisly sound of crunching bones filled the desolate alleyway.

As the siren faded into the distance, the woman released Ronny. The little that was left of his lifeless body crumpled to the ground, reduced to a bloody heap.

She licked her glistening lips.

The woman turned away, her silhouette disappearing back into the mist.

And so, Kitten Heels carried on as usual—the music played, the girls danced, and the patrons drank, each lost in their own world of fleeting pleasures.

Outside, however, darkness had just claimed a victim, a prelude to the nightmare descending on Paradise Falls.

C

CHAPTER FIVE

You have summoned me. I rise again.

Zane was restless all night long. The words kept replaying in his head. When morning came, a fog had descended, clouding everything.

The more he thought about the ritual they had performed the night before, the more he panicked. *What did we do?*

A long shower didn't help much. He moved through the rest of his morning routine feeling every bit as foggy as the world outside his window.

In the kitchen, he turned on an old portable TV his uncle had left behind. It was a relic from the '80s that only picked up a few local channels. Still, Zane liked having the background noise while he ate breakfast.

He poured himself a bowl of cereal, but he didn't have

much of an appetite. He sat at the table, staring blankly as the marshmallows in the cereal turned the milk green.

A breaking news alert flashed across the TV screen:

"…Reporting live from downtown Paradise Falls, at the scene of one of three brutal murders that have left this community reeling. Three men were violently murdered last night, their bodies discovered at different locations across town, including here at Kitten Heels, a popular adult entertainment club. Authorities have described the scenes as gruesome, with the victims' bodies partially consumed and ravaged beyond recognition. It is unclear at this time if these killings are related to additional reports of two local area men who went missing last night. Police are urging residents to remain vigilant and report any suspicious activity. More on this story as it develops…"

Zane's stomach dropped. Was it all connected? He pushed his breakfast aside, grabbed his skateboard, and rushed to work. He needed to talk to Star and Dexter.

Zane found his friends together in the back of the kitchen.

"I told you we shouldn't have done that ritual again." Dexter shook his head. He was pale. "I mean, do you think... Do you think these murders have something to do with it?"

Zane sighed, "It's too much of a coincidence."

"You guys heard that voice, too." Dexter was wild-eyed.

"We straight-up *summoned* something—something *evil*—and now there's blood on our hands!"

"Okay." Star tried to calm Dexter down. "We don't know anything. Sure, we all *thought* we heard something, but it was late, we're all tired, and honestly, I don't even know what happened here last night. Let's not assume the worst. We should go back to the book and look for answers."

"What part of SUMMONED and EVIL do you not understand?" Dexter punctuated each word by chopping his hands together.

"Okay, let's say we did, like, 'summon' some kind of 'evil monster' or whatever..." Star made air quotes as she spoke. "Then we have to do *something* about it, right? If we started this, maybe we're the only ones who can stop it."

"Ay, Dios mío," Dexter groaned, turning around to bang his head against the wall. "Where would we even start? We're in way over our heads."

"The answers are in Harold Snaxton's journal." Zane knew it.

Jake strutted into the kitchen and flashed a bright smile. "What's the secret huddle all about?"

"Oh, you know..." Star hesitated, not wanting to drag him into whatever they might have unleashed—especially since Jake had made it very clear he wanted nothing to do with the journal. "Dexter's just going on about his Pokémon obsession... for the *millionth* time."

Dexter glared at Star. He hadn't mentioned his Pokémon collection in weeks.

Jake lowered his voice. "So, did you guys hear about those murders last night?"

"Yeah, pretty messed up," Zane said.

Jake squinted. "And all this weird stuff happening here at Snaxtime this past week... Wait, you guys aren't still messin' with that recipe book, are you?"

"OMG, like, totally not," Star's valley girl accent was more pronounced than usual. "It's just Mercury in retrograde. That's always a hot mess."

"Mercury *what* now?" Jake scratched the back of his neck. He looked around as if expecting someone to be eavesdropping and whispered, "Honestly, between us, all these murders… I'll be sleeping with one eye open, that's for sure."

Dexter, the smallest guy in the room, looked up at Jake. "Dude, you're built like a tank. What could possibly shake *you*?"

Jake flexed his bicep. "You know what they say, the hot guy always gets killed off first."

Star scoffed. "*Nobody* says that."

Jake winked. "Well, I just did." He turned and strolled away.

They waited for him to be out of earshot. "Tonight," Zane said quietly, "we meet up and figure this out."

Star agreed, "Totally. We've got, like, the future of

Paradise Falls in our hands."

"Or the world," Zane added

"Well, when you put it that way..." Dexter reached his arms around them and pulled them close. "Can't let you guys go down in history for saving the world without me."

That night, Zane waited for Star and Dexter in the break room. A signed picture of Harold Snaxton hung on the wall. Zane had passed by the portrait a hundred times without thinking about it. But tonight, Harold's eyes looked alive, like they were watching him.

Zane stepped closer. Harold was smiling with his arms crossed. His bright red hair and orange mustache made him look like a cross between Colonel Sanders and Ronald McDonald. The founder's signature at the bottom of the portrait was penned in the same cursive script as the journal's.

"Okay, let's get back to it," Star suggested as she and Dexter entered the room together.

"Can't wait to see what we summon tonight," Dexter remarked.

With the book open on the table in front of them, they dug right in. Time slipped away without finding anything useful.

Then Dexter noticed something new—an unfamiliar page. "Whoa, what's this?"

A drawing showed a woman with long, flowing hair. Around her were lifeless men, naked. Wisps of something, like spirits, rose from their mouths and spiraled into hers.

"Um, how have we never seen this before?" Star asked.

"It's like it was hidden," Dexter said.

"Or like we unlocked it," Zane added.

Star looked at the text under the image. "It's about a demon—a seductress who used her beauty to trap men and steal their souls.

"Well, that's reassuring," Dexter snarked.

"She was stunning," Star continued. "Like, so unbelievably gorgeous that men would willingly give their lives for just one look at her. Once she had them under her spell, she'd drain their souls, using them to fuel her power. Her name was Demonika—a dark queen from the depths of Hell."

"*Demonika?*" Dexter made a face. "Sounds like something straight out of a low-budget B-movie."

But the reality of their situation crashed down on them like a tidal wave.

"We screwed up big time, didn't we?" Dexter, for once, wasn't joking around.

"Yeah, we did," Star whispered.

They kept reading, diving into the twisted story of an ancient demon. This entity was older than most of humanity's earliest records. She was a primal force that reveled in chaos and destruction. If awakened from her deep slumber, she would unleash terror upon the world, unless stopped and sealed back in her tomb.

One passage spoke of a time centuries ago when Paradise Falls was the battleground against this relentless fiend:

Dreadful days fell upon the hamlet of Paradise Falls. Townsmen, once the sturdy pillars of this close-knit community, were felled one after another, victims of a force beyond their comprehension. Families were shattered, and the town became a husk of its former glory. This period marked the demon's rise, initiating an age fraught with turmoil yet significant change.

However, this phase of darkness was not destined to endure. A ritual of banishment quelled Demonika's rule. The specifics of this ceremony...

They flipped ahead. But the critical details of the banishment ritual were absent. The following pages were empty.

"So let me get this straight," Dexter started. "We're dealing with a demonic force more formidable than anything we could ever imagine, and the roadmap to defeating her is a blank page."

"Looks like we have our work cut out for us," Star remarked. "We *need* that ritual."

Star was right.

Dexter searched on his phone for anything related to demons or paranormal activity in Paradise Falls, but found nothing.

Star had a thought. "What about the library? They keep all the old town records there, right?"

"Man, the library?" Dexter groaned. "I mean, I guess a lot of the great supernatural adventures start there— *Ghostbusters, Harry Potter, Buffy the Vampire Slayer...*"

"Buffy's totally my hero," Star added.

"Let's hit the books tomorrow morning," Zane agreed.

Zane dragged himself to the curb at 7:45 AM, weary from another restless night. His stomach growled, protesting the skipped breakfast.

Star pulled up in her powder blue Buick. Dexter rolled down the passenger window. He was annoyingly alert. "Wow, Zane," he quipped with his gap-toothed grin. "I didn't realize the Crypt Keeper had a younger brother."

In haste, Zane hadn't even glanced in the mirror that morning. "Good to see you too, sunshine. Your radiant cheer is blinding," Zane retorted. He slid into the back seat, yawning while trying to smooth down his unkempt hair.

"Morning, Sleepyhead," Star teased. "Fasten your seatbelts. Next stop, the library."

The town's library was established in the late 19th century. It was distinguished by its red bricks, stained-glass windows, white columns, and a grand wooden door.

"Never been in one of these before," Dexter joked.

Star cracked a smile. "Geez, Dex, aren't you supposed to be a nerd or something?"

The library was deserted. It smelled like lemon polish oil and old books.

"Good morning," a librarian greeted them from behind a book.

"Good morning, Mrs. English," Star replied with a smile, clearly familiar with her.

Zane and Dexter exchanged a puzzled glance.

The woman looked up. "Oh, hello, Star! What a wonderful surprise! And I see you've brought some friends." She smiled at them before adding, "Did you boys know that Star was Paradise Falls' youth trivia champion three years in a row?"

"No, we didn't!" Dexter answered. He turned to Star. "Who's the nerd, now?"

"Tell us more," Zane encouraged.

"Oh, she was unstoppable! I used to joke that we should just engrave her name on the trophy permanently. Smart as a whip and quick with those answers. I still talk about her to this day!"

"And I owe it all to the best librarian in the entire world!" Star played the teacher's pet role effortlessly.

"So, what brings you kids into the library on such a beautiful summer morning?" the librarian inquired. "It sure is early."

"Tell me about it," Zane mumbled with a yawn.

"Yep, we're off to an early start today," Star said.

"Well, I do always say, the early bird gets the *bookworm*." She chuckled to herself.

"Good one, Mrs. Librarian," Dexter approved.

"We're looking for old newspapers," Zane replied.

"Ah," she said, pointing to a corner with outdated-looking computers. "Those stations over there have everything from 2000 onward. But anything earlier wasn't digitized. It's all on microfiche, located on the lower level."

Dexter elbowed Star lightly. "Micro-fish? What's that?"

"Beats me, I just come here for the paperbacks," Star responded with a shrug.

Zane was equally clueless.

The librarian was amused. "Oh, I should've guessed. We stopped using microfiche ages ago—long before you were even born. Here, come with me. I'll show you how to use it."

She led them down to a room with long rows of metal cabinets. Strips of lights encased in metal cages hung from the ceiling.

"These cabinets," she gestured, "contain all the newspaper archives. They're organized and labeled by date."

After a brief demo on the microfiche machines, the librarian left them to start their research. The trio split up, each taking on a different cabinet. They began scouring through the archives, their eyes scanning labels and fingers flicking through the microfilm sheets.

Dexter called out from his corner with excitement. "Check this out!" He held up a sheet, squinting at the small print.

Star and Zane gathered around him as he inserted the slide into the viewer. The screen illuminated a newspaper article from the *Paradise Record*, dating back to 1949.

"'Snaxtime Grand Opening Marks a New Era for Paradise Falls,'" Dexter read aloud. "'The opening of Snaxtime, the town's first drive-in restaurant, was celebrated with a grand ribbon-cutting ceremony. Attended by town dignitaries...'"

Star enlarged a photo showing Harold Snaxton with the mayor and Miss Paradise Falls. She was wearing a sash and holding an oversized pair of scissors. "Wait, that's my Grammy! She was Miss Paradise Falls 1949!"

"Wait," Dexter blurted. "You've got beauty queen blood and never thought to share? What else are you keeping from us, Star?"

Star executed a flawless pageant wave with a smile as bright as stage lights. "Oh, I just thought that was, like, totally obvious."

"Maybe we should talk to your grandmother," Zane suggested. "She might remember something about Harold Snaxton or the town back then."

Star nodded. "Yeah, we could try. Grammy's pretty out of it these days, though. She might not remember much from that long ago." Then she turned back to Dexter. "So, what else does the article say?"

Dexter continued, "'The opening of Snaxtime has stirred debate among residents. The establishment stands on the site of the New Hope Fellowship Church, which was destroyed by fire last year. Many community members have voiced concern about the loss of a significant part of the town's history...'"

Zane looked over Dexter's shoulder. "Wow, so Snaxtime's built on a church site, huh?"

"Let's keep looking and see what else we can find," Star pressed.

Hours went by, and their determination faded. The sound of rustling microfiche and the soft clicking of the viewing machines became a monotonous soundtrack.

"Whoa!" Zane exclaimed.

Star and Dexter hurried over. Zane had found an article from 1978. "The headline's about a bunch of unsolved murders here in town."

"Unsolved murders? What does it say?" Dexter asked.

Zane adjusted the focus and read aloud, "'A mysterious string of homicides has left Paradise Falls in fear. The culprit remains at large...'" He skimmed. "All victims were male... there were no suspects..."

"That sounds an awful lot like what happened here the other night," Dexter said.

"This is super creepy." Star cringed. "Does it say anything else?"

Zane advanced to the next page. "Oh, check this, they brought in a psychic to help with the investigation—Viola Beaumont."

"Our first real lead!" Star's fingers were already flying over her phone. "Let's see what we can dig up on this Viola Beaumont psychic lady... Found something!" She held up her phone to show them a website for a local psychic parlor called Enchanted Realms. "It's run by a woman named Madame Viola. That's gotta be her, right?"

Zane glanced at the time. The day was still young, and they had just stumbled upon a potentially significant clue. "Let's pay her a visit."

"But wait..." Dexter's stomach grumbled. "Anyone else starving?"

Star smacked her lips. "Actually, I could totally demolish some pancakes right now. The Pancake House on Main Street has the best boysenberry syrup."

"You're speakin' my language." Dexter said.

The Pancake House was a nostalgic restaurant chain known for its round-the-clock breakfast. Squishy green leather booths lined the walls and the red-and-white checkered floor was worn but freshly mopped.

A server, balancing an overflowing tray of food, greeted Zane, Star, and Dexter. "Sit wherever you want. I'll be with you in a minute."

"Thanks," Star replied, tugging her friends to a sunny booth by the window.

"I'm hungrier than an elephant in a peanut factory," Dexter said while grabbing a menu.

"What does that even mean?" Star sighed.

"Well, you know. Elephants like peanuts, right?" Dexter responded.

Zane jumped in, "Ha, yeah. Dumbo sure loved 'em."

"Oh my God, what is this? Like, first grade?" Star grabbed the menu from Dexter's hands.

A young waiter approached with three red plastic cups of water with pellet ice. He had a fuzzy mustache and a well-kept mullet. "Hi, welcome to Pancake House. I'm Travis, and I'll be your server today. Do you need a min…?"

"I'm ready!" Dexter shouted. "I'll have the Hungry Boy Special. Chocolate chip pancakes, scrambled eggs, add cheese, hash browns, extra crispy. And the sausage… is it patties or links?"

"Links," Travis replied with a nod.

"Hmm, I prefer patties, but links will do."

The waiter smiled, scribbling the order down on his pad. "How 'bout some whipped cream on your pancakes?"

"You read my mind! Oh, and a strawberry shake too."

Dexter patted his belly while glancing sideways toward Star. "I'll *start* with that."

Not amused, Star ordered next. "I'll have a short stack and a Diet Coke, extra ice. Thanks."

"You got it." The waiter turned to Zane. "And for you?"

"Um, I'll just have a tuna melt with fries. And a coffee."

"You got it," The waiter repeated. "I'll be right back with your drinks."

"Man, you could totally rock a mullet like that," Dexter teased Zane after the waiter left.

"Meh, not my style, but I've always wanted to try a stache," Zane replied, half-joking.

"Ew, gross, no. Don't," Star interjected, scrunching her nose. "Stick to your current look — it's working for you."

"Well, *I* think it'd be sexy. Sign me up," Dexter said with a suggestive wiggle of his eyebrows.

Zane patted him on the shoulder. "I think we should just be friends, Dex."

"Ouch, friend-zoned!"

"Okay, let's check out Madame Viola's website," Star said, bringing her phone close to her face. "Wow, this site is like a hundred years old." Her thumb scrolled through the page. "Oh my God, do you think she already knows we're coming?"

Dexter snickered at the thought. "It would be quite the endorsement for her psychic abilities."

The waiter returned with their drinks.

Zane cradled the hot coffee mug between his hands. "So, what does the site say? Does it mention anything about her solving a satanic murder mystery from the '70s?"

Star flicked her eyes up from her phone. "Let me see…. Nope, nothing about banishing a demon serial killer." She paused. "Oh, this is interesting. She used to host one of those old psychic hotline shows. Oh my God, it's *soooo* old, like from the '90s. Super low budget. There's a whole playlist of episodes!"

Star clicked on a video and positioned her screen so they could all watch it. In the fuzzy clip, Madame Viola sat behind a large pink crystal ball, with layers of velvet curtains draped around the gaudy set. A bold yellow 1-900 number flashed at the bottom.

Madame Viola was a sight to behold. She wore a turquoise silk blouse with ruffles, boxy glasses tinted pink and purple, and a turban with wisps of black hair peeking out. Large earrings and several rings accessorized her outfit. Her red lipstick and long red nails looked oversaturated under the studio lights.

In the episode, a caller's voice came through with a midwestern drawl. "Um, hello, Madame Viola?" She began with nervousness in her voice. "So last week, I, uh, tried using a Ouija board to reach out to my Aunt Edna, who passed away quite suddenly. I thought I could… Well, you know, talk to her again." She let out a shaky breath before continuing. "And I'm pretty sure it worked. The board said it was her, which I believed at first. But now I don't know…

"Since that night, some real weird stuff has been happening around the house. I've been hearing strange noises, like scratches and footsteps, when there's nobody else around, and I swear things are being moved around when I'm not looking. It's starting to freak me out, and I don't know what to do..."

"Oh, sweetheart," Madame Viola responded in a thick, smoky accent. "Ouija boards can open doors better left closed. They invite energies we don't wish to deal with. I've had my fair share of encounters with demonic forces, and trust me, it's not something you want to mess around with."

She guided the caller on cleansing the house, starting with burying the Ouija board and burning sage.

Madame Viola then shifted gears, her voice dropping lower. "But darling, there's a sweet presence watching over you right now. Does the name Francine mean anything to you?"

A gasp rang out over the line, followed by a choked sob. "Franny," the caller whimpered, "My little Franny. She was my miniature white poodle. I… I just lost her in March."

Madame Viola reassured the caller. "She's just fine, sweetheart. And she's surrounded by all the muffins her little heart could ever desire."

"Oh wow, I gave her a blueberry muffin every Sunday. Bless her little heart. And thank you, Madame Viola!"

Star paused the video.

"I could sure go for one of Franny's blueberry muffins right about now," Dexter chuckled.

Star raised her Diet Coke. "To Franny."

"To Franny," Zane and Dexter said in unison as they clinked their drinks together.

"So, the fate of humanity really rests on the shoulders of a TV psychic who talks to dead poodles?" Dexter questioned.

"It's sure looking that way." Zane surrendered, taking a sip of his coffee.

The server came back, arms overflowing with an extravagant spread.

"Oh my God, finally, I'm literally starving." Star's pancakes soaked up the boysenberry syrup she generously drizzled over them.

Dexter's meal was a veritable tower of breakfast decadence—the pancakes were packed with chocolate chips, crowned with a cloud of whipped cream, and dusted with powdered sugar. The large, greasy plate beside it was piled with scrambled eggs, covered in gooey cheese, crispy hash browns, and two plump sausages.

Zane's overly stuffed tuna melt and heap of fries looked downright sensible next to Dexter's meal.

Dexter doused his pancakes with butter-pecan-flavored syrup. "Oh," he began, shoveling a forkful of cheesy eggs into his mouth. "Did I ever tell you about the time I used a Ouija board with my four-year-old twin cousins on

Halloween?"

"Um, no, but this should be good," Star replied, settling in with her Diet Coke.

"So," His eyes twinkled with mischief. "It's Halloween, right? And I'm babysitting little Benito and Bobby overnight. They're all dressed up—cute little red devils, pitchforks and all—and they're super excited about their first proper trick-or-treating adventure.

"I was dressed as Donatello, not the Italian sculpture dude, but the famous turtle. You know, the highly trained Ninja Turtle and savvy tech genius of the group. I even had a bo staff, his weapon of choice. But I digress…

"So we go around the neighborhood, gather a motherlode of candy, and head back home." Dexter took a moment to devour a large chunk of pancakes before continuing, "I propose a 'fun game of Ouija board' to round out the night. I mean, what's Halloween without a ghost story, right?"

"Poor kids," Star interrupted, "that's too scary. They were *FOUR!*"

"A bit scary, sure. But they were more intrigued, especially when I said we might contact the Candy Ghost, who could double their candy stash instantly."

Zane snorted, nearly choking on his coffee, "You didn't."

"Oh, I did." Dexter grinned like a Cheshire cat as he savored a bite of sausage. "And you should have seen their faces when the pointer started moving! And then I told them we accidentally contacted the wrong ghost, the spirit of a little girl who died on Halloween. She spelled out: *GIVE ME ALL YOUR CANDY OR DIE.* Their eyes went as big as frisbees. They dropped their bags of candy and ran out of the room screaming like babies!"

Star's jaw dropped. "You *didn't* take their candy, Dexter!"

"I prefer to think I saved their precious little teeth from a trip to the dentist," he said with a wily wink. "But then, the twist of the century happened..."

"Don't tell me. The dead little girl was real?" Zane asked.

"Well, let's just say that things got a little freaky at midnight. I'm in the guest room, in bed, surrounded by candy wrappers. And out of nowhere, there was this crazy scratching sound at the window. It started out kind of soft, but it kept getting louder, and it wouldn't stop. I'd go to the window, and nothing would be there, but it would start again as soon as I got back into bed. I swear it went on for, like, an hour.

"And then, I heard it. The unmistakable giggle of a little girl. First, it came from the window, then from the hallway outside my door! Suddenly, there are footsteps all around and banging on the door." Dexter's face fell dramatically, mimicking horror. "There I am, under my covers on the verge of tears, convinced that my little prank had summoned a real ghost!"

"And?" Star prodded, enthralled despite herself.

"Next thing I know, the door slams open, and it sounds like a stampede's coming my way! I can feel something, or *someone*, climbing into bed with me. I whip off the sheets and let out a scream like I'm meeting my maker right then and there. But, nope, no spooky little ghost girl in sight. Guess who it was? Benito and Bobby, the little rascals! They had snuck out of their room and were pulling my leg, all to snatch back their candy!"

Dexter shook his head, his face beaming as he pinched a fry off Zane's plate. "The little devils scared the crap out of me!"

Star waved a syrupy fork in his direction. "Well, you got what you deserved. I like these kids."

Unabashed, Dexter swallowed his last bite and grinned, revealing a glop of chocolate stuck in the gap of his teeth. Fixated on Star's half-eaten pancakes, he inquired, "You gonna finish that?"

Star pushed her plate across the table. "Your stomach is literally a black hole."

"Well, they do call me the Cheese Dog King!" Dexter proclaimed while stuffing the rest of Star's pancakes into his mouth.

Star rolled her eyes. "Oh, is that right? You'll have to tell me that story sometime."

Zane stretched in his seat as he picked up the check that the waiter had left them. "Alright, you two. Let's get moving."

C

CHAPTER SIX

Madame Viola's house was dusty purple with bright pink trim. The scalloped roof and stone chimney were in perfect condition, and the lush garden surrounding the house was neatly tended. A tall rock wall enclosed the property, and an ornate iron gate stood at the entrance, welcoming visitors into the well-kept setting.

Inside, Madame Viola was reclining on her floral couch watching the Home Shopping Channel. A regal Siamese cat sat on her lap.

The psychic's gnarled hand, decorated with an assortment of cocktail rings, glided over the cat's sleek fur. With her other hand, she brought a slim cigarette to her glossed lips. The smoke mingled with the scent of burning incense.

Her black hair, streaked with thick white strands, was

styled on top of her head. Her face was round and wrinkled. Oversized glasses sat on her nose, and her honey-colored eyes still had a youthful spark despite her age.

The parlor, which also served as Madame Viola's place of business, was filled with curios and trinkets collected over decades. Each item had a story, a purpose, and a place of its own. Shelves upon shelves of potions, elixirs, and serums lined the walls, while assorted crystals and charms were strategically placed.

Persian rugs were scattered across the wooden floor. Velvet furniture was decorated with beaded pillows and throws. Heavy curtains shielded the interior from prying eyes.

It had been a slow week for Madame Viola. Only a few palm and tarot readings broke up her solitude. In her heyday, she was a popular TV personality and a well-known figure in town, with many seeking her services. But now, she led a quieter life.

The crunch of gravel in the driveway pulled Madame Viola from her reminiscence. She stubbed out her cigarette and rose from the couch with the assistance of a jewel-topped walking stick. She was swathed in a flowy, embroidered caftan that dragged on the floor. This gave her the appearance of levitating slightly above the ground as she walked. Her jewelry chimed and jangled as she moved.

She ambled over to the window and pulled open the curtain to reveal a trio of teenagers emerging from a car. A pretty redhead girl, hair flaming like the setting sun, was flanked by two boys.

Madame Viola smiled. It wasn't often that she had such young visitors. She turned off the television and put on a CD of New Age music.

She checked her reflection in the mirror. With practiced ease, she fluffed her hair into place.

The door opened with a jingle of dangling charms.

"Greetings, curious souls!" Madame Viola exclaimed with a theatrical flourish of her hand. "And welcome to Enchanted Realms, the House of Secrets and Revelations!"

The trio stepped inside.

"Whoa." Dexter was entranced, his attention darting from one artifact to another. Madame Viola's cat brushed against his legs. "Hey, little buddy." He ran his hand down its back.

"I am Madame Viola, the Seer of the Unseen, Keeper of the Unknown! Allow me to unveil the mysteries of the cosmos and peer into the veils of your destiny! Would anyone like a palm reading? Tarot, perhaps?"

Dexter picked up a bottle from a shelf lined with serums and elixirs, reading the label with curiosity.

"Over here," the psychic called, guiding them toward a table and motioning for them to sit. A large crystal ball dominated the tabletop.

They settled into their seats. Madame Viola lowered herself into her chair and interlocked her fingers on the table. The crystal ball magnified the sparkle of her rings.

"What draws you here, children?" she inquired.

Zane cleared his throat. "Hello, Madame Viola. I'm Zane and these are my friends, Star and Dexter. We were wondering if maybe you could help us."

"A pleasure to make your acquaintance." Her eyes penetrated Zane's. Surprise flashed across her face. "Remarkable... It's rare to see a golden aura as brilliant as yours."

Zane shifted, unsure. "Oh, um..."

"It's a symbol of spiritual enlightenment and celestial shielding. You have an angel watching over you."

Dexter raised his hand. "What about my aura?"

"You, young man, radiate a turquoise hue. It signifies a cheerful disposition, and..."

Star cut in, "We're not here for an aura reading, Madame Viola. We really need your help, and it's, like, super urgent."

Zane added, "We were hoping to learn more about a bunch of unsolved murders from the '70s here in Paradise Falls."

Star pulled out her phone and opened a picture she'd taken of the newspaper article. She pushed it across the table toward Viola. "It says that you were there."

Madame Viola's eyes darted from the phone to the expectant faces around the table. "Why on Earth would you be interested in something that happened before you kids were even born?" she asked dismissively.

"Well, you might've heard about the murders in town," Zane began. "We kinda think there might be a connection."

"A connection? With an event that happened decades ago?" She was caught off guard.

"We think so," Dexter said. "The circumstances are... weird. Similar."

Madame Viola let out a laugh that didn't quite reach her eyes. "Oh, you're overthinking it," she scoffed, flipping a hand. "It's easy to draw lines where there aren't any."

"But, like, there totally *are* connections, Madame Viola," Star interjected. "Something really bad is happening. And we... we just need to stop it."

For a moment, Viola's flamboyant facade faded, revealing a glimmer of something deeper. "Oh, that's just silly now. Why would you want to dig up such old horrors?" she replied with feigned nonchalance. "You should be enjoying your youth. The Paradise Falls Carnival is just around the corner. Isn't that something you should be looking forward to? Now how about that tarot reading?"

"There's more." Zane reached into his backpack and pulled out the journal. He placed it onto the table with a thud.

Madame Viola's eyes bulged in recognition. "*Where* did you get that book?!" Her voice was quivering.

"We found it at work… We work at Snaxtime," Zane explained. "It belonged to the founder, Harold Snaxton. It's filled with spells. We're worried that we might have… "

"What did you do?! Get out!" she shrieked. "Get that book out of my house! *NOW!*"

Her outburst startled them, and they stumbled out of their seats. Zane grabbed the journal. As she rushed them out the door, Madame Viola's warnings followed them. "Burn that book! Burn it and bury it!"

She slammed the door behind them and locked it. With trembling hands, she flipped the "Closed" sign and drew the curtains, leaving only a sliver of a gap through which she could watch them retreat.

Madame Viola's world turned inside out as the memories flooded in. There was a time when she battled an unspeakable evil. She had worked hard to bury that traumatic past.

Familiar dread consumed her. With a sinking heart, she realized the journal was indeed the origin of the recent horror that had plagued Paradise Falls. Her chest tightened.

Urgency pushed her into action. She scurried across the room to her vials, trinkets, and objects. She grabbed several white candles, amulets, and a collection of herbs and oils.

Viola picked up her treasured grimoire, a book filled with her notes on spells and rituals she had performed over the years.

Stooping to the floor, she began her preparations. She arranged the candles in a precise circle around her and placed a brass bowl in the center. Above, a crucifix hung on the wall. After lighting the candles, she filled the bowl with the collected ingredients and set them ablaze. Sweet, fragrant smoke spiraled upward.

She opened the book and read from it. "Let no evil pass this boundary," she breathed into the smoky air. "Let no evil pass this boundary…" She repeated the phrase.

The only witness to the ritual was her feline familiar, watching intently from his velvet cushion. He hissed, staring at a corner of the room now hidden by the swirling ritual smoke.

In response to the cat's reaction, Madame Viola shifted her chant to an ancient language. "*Nozhal vrohk dhizbrin.*"

The crucifix fell from the wall and clattered onto the hardwood floor.

She gasped.

"*NOZHAL VROHK DHIZBRIN… NOZHAL VROHK DHIZBRIN!*" Her television zapped to life. The sound blasted at a deafening volume, drowning out her voice.

A tornado descended upon the room. Books ripped from the shelves and flew through the air. Pillows flung from the couch. Glass containers of serums and potions exploded in a shower of shards. A burst of sparks erupted from the power outlet.

The room plunged into darkness.

Only the glow from the still-burning bowl provided any illumination.

Silence.

Madame Viola clutched at her chest, gasping for breath. A ghostly whisper emerged from the walls and slithered into her ears. She spun around on her knees. The cat continued to growl at the shadowy corner of the room.

Then Viola saw it. The demon had returned.

"You!" This was an entity she had hoped never to encounter again.

It knocked her off her knees to the floor.

The temperature dropped. The room was freezing.

It laughed at her.

The psychic got up and tried to run away, but her numb legs buckled beneath her. She dragged herself along the floor, ripping her fingernails as she clawed for traction.

She felt its weight as it mounted her.

Images of the three teenagers filled her mind. They were innocent yet now caught in this ancient web of evil. Her fear for them overshadowed her own terror.

She realized with regret that Harold Snaxton's journal was crucial. It was not only used to summon the demon but also essential for sending her back. She wondered if her hasty instruction to destroy the book had been a grave mistake. She should have burned it herself decades ago.

Her vision faded to a blur. She gasped for air as her strength drained away.

Her last thought, a silent prayer, was that the kids would find the path of protection and stop Demonika from being brought back permanently.

She surrendered.

The quiet that followed seemed almost sacrilegious, given what had occurred. Madame Viola lay still on the floor, her frozen face contorted in fear.

CHAPTER SEVEN

Paradise Falls was blasted with a summer heat that felt like opening an oven door. At Snaxtime, the lunchtime rush was in full swing. As the temperature climbed, so did the number of people seeking air conditioning and a bite to eat.

Dexter pulled Star and Zane aside in the kitchen. Madame Viola's warning hung over them like a storm cloud. "I can't stop thinking about what happened yesterday. I mean, Madame Viola was, like, totally freaked out. What do we do now?"

"We'll figure it out," Star assured him. "But yeah, it's getting super scary, for real."

"D'you think we should burn the book? That's what she told us to do," Zane reminded them.

"No way!" Star responded. "We need the book to reverse whatever we did. It's all we have."

Dexter wasn't convinced. "Seriously, guys, think about it. Madame Viola knows this stuff, and she was scared out of her mind. If she says burn it, we should."

Star crossed her arms. "Um, hello? Just burn it and everything's suddenly fine? We messed up big time. If we ditch the book, we lose our only shot at fixing this."

Zane scratched the back of his head. "But if keeping the book means that more people die…"

Dexter shook his head, adamant. "We can't play around. Burning it is the safest bet."

Star got louder. "*Safe*? Oh my God, Dexter, we're way past safe! That book is the key, and you just wanna torch it?"

Zane weighed the options. "Maybe there *is* something in the book."

Dexter clenched his hands into fists. "All it's brought is mayhem, death... and did you forget about the maggots? Why are we still holding onto it? What if we make things even worse, huh? Did you think about that?"

Star stood her ground. "Then we figure it out."

Dexter wasn't having it. "I say we listen to the one person who knows what she's talking about... MADAME VIOLA!"

"Guys, keep your heads down," Zane noticed Marjorie heading toward them. "Marjorie, three o'clock."

"Are you talking about Madame Viola?" Marjorie asked as she walked up to them.

"Uh, yeah?" Zane wasn't sure how much she had overheard.

Marjorie shook her head. "Such a shame."

"What do you mean? You know Madame Viola??" Dexter asked.

"Weren't you talking about the murder?"

"Murder?!" they all said in unison.

"I'm confused," Marjorie said. "I thought you were talking about the town psychic. It's been all over the news. She was killed last night."

"Oh my God, WHAT?!" Star exclaimed. "What happened?"

Marjorie shrugged, "I don't know. The neighbors called the police because they heard a bunch of commotion. Last I heard, they were still investigating."

The world spun a little slower.

"So, why were you talking about her then?" Marjorie asked.

"Oh, we, uh," Zane stumbled over his words. "We actually saw her yesterday. For a reading..."

"Yeah," Star continued. "We thought it would be fun or whatever."

"Wow, really?!" Marjorie was shocked by the coincidence. "Did you talk to the police? Did you see anything weird while you were there?"

The teenagers shook their heads, denial coming out a little too quickly.

Dexter couldn't keep his composure. "I think I'm gonna throw up."

Marjorie rubbed his back. "Oh my God, are you okay, honey?"

"I think we just need a minute," Star said.

"Alright." Marjorie paused at the kitchen door. "But don't dilly-dally too much," she added, checking her watch before leaving. "It's busy out there."

Dexter was on edge. "Guys, I'm seriously freaking out. Should we go to the police?"

"Relax, Dex," Star said. "We're all shook, but we've got to keep it together. And what would we even tell the cops, anyway? 'Oh, hi, officers! So, my friends and I totally summoned an ancient demon from some dusty old cookbook, and now she's, like, gone all serial killer on the town'? They'd have us in straitjackets the second we said 'demon.'"

"Or worse," Zane added. "They'd pin these murders on us. Trust me, I've dealt with my fair share of cops. They're not gonna help us find the banishing ritual, that's for sure. And if they lock us up, who's going to put an end to all of this?"

"Fine. So, what's our plan, then? Are we keeping the journal or what?" Dexter pressed.

"Absolutely, we need that book," Star committed. "Right, Zane?"

Zane was uncertain.

From the front, Marjorie shouted, "Zane, open up Register Three!"

"Yes, Ma'am!" Zane turned to his friends. "Let's pick this up later." He moved to the register and announced, "Next!"

A guy in a biker jacket, about Zane's age, walked up to the counter. His hair was spiky and bleached, and a silver crescent moon dangled from his ear. He had pouty lips and impossibly green eyes. He looked like something out of a dream.

Zane was breathless for a moment. He plastered on his practiced customer service smile, uttering the standard greeting, "Welcome to Snaxtime. Would you like to try a Cheesy Double Dog Combo with Mega Cheesy Tots and Super Sip Soda?"

"Oh, I have never been here before," the customer confessed. His voice was deep. "What is good?"

"Well, you can't go wrong with the Cheesy Double Dog Combo. But pro tip, the Crispy Beef Tacos are killer. And the Jalapeño Hot Bites are pretty sick, too. Top it all off with an Orange Gush, you won't regret it. Oh, and get a side of chipotle ranch with the poppers instead of sour cream." *Stop rambling.* "If you like dessert, the Pineapple Party Cake is my go-to. Skip the flan—I mean, it's not bad, but..." *Shut up, Zane.*

"Whatever you say," the guy said with an easy grin.

"Okay, how 'bout the tacos, bites, and an Orange Gush?"

"Don't forget that chipotle ranch."

Zane blushed. "You know it." He fumbled as he entered the order. "How about dessert?"

"Maybe next time."

"Okay, that'll be $12.49," he gulped. "For here or to go?"

"For here," the patron replied, offering up cash.

Preparing the order was a blur. Zane served the tray and watched as the young man walked to a secluded booth. There was something about him. He seemed so familiar.

Who are you?

The guy ate, never once glancing back at Zane, who, between serving other customers, snuck peeks in his direction.

Eventually, the stranger stood up and cleared his tray. He approached the counter on his way to the exit.

"You are correct, the tacos are indeed *killer*. Thank you."

"Yeah, right? I'm so glad you liked 'em." There was a weird energy between them. "Have we...?"

"Nice to meet you, Zane. They call me Hunter."

Before Zane could respond, he was gone.

Hunter.

Zane left the register and went back to the kitchen to compose himself. His heart was pounding.

"Zane, Earth to Zane," Dexter waved a hand in front of his face.

Star crossed her arms. "Yeah, snap out of it. That guy was, like, super intense."

"How'd he know my name?" Zane wondered aloud.

Star poked at his name tag. "Um, duh, it says it right there."

Zane looked down at his chest. *I'm losing it.*

"What was all that about?" Star asked.

Trying to dismiss the unexplained attraction he had experienced, Zane shrugged. "Nothin', just some dude."

As the words left his mouth, he knew he was not being entirely honest, not to his friends and certainly not to himself.

"Well, he kinda gave me the creeps." Star was clearly a little jealous.

"So yeah, what's our next move?" Zane changed the subject, hoping to steer the conversation away from Hunter and back to their collective predicament.

Dexter yawned. "Honestly, I don't know about you guys, but I barely slept last night. I could really catch some Zs after work."

"Totally." Star popped her gum. "Let's power through today and recharge tonight. Maybe by tomorrow morning, we'll know more about Madame Viola."

They got back to work. As the day wore on, Zane couldn't stop thinking about Hunter.

It was well after midnight, and Zane was wide awake. He sprawled on his bed with an arm tucked under his head.

It was too hot for a real pillow. Shirtless, his sweaty skin gleamed under the moonlight filtering through his blinds.

His mind was a whirlpool—thoughts of the slain men, Madame Viola, and Hunter swirled. The Sandman, it seemed, would not be visiting him tonight.

Snaxton's journal taunted him from the nightstand. He could open it to look for more clues, but he really needed sleep. Or maybe a shower would clear his head. He pushed himself off the bed and shuffled across the carpet to the bathroom.

The chilly tiles felt soothing against the soles of his feet. Zane slipped off his boxers and looked at himself in the mirror. His hair was untamed, and he had dark circles under his eyes. "Man, you're a mess," he whispered to his counterpart, gripping the porcelain sink.

He stepped into the shower. The cool water was a delicious relief. He lathered a bar of soap across his skin. It was so refreshing, exactly what he needed. The water turned even colder. But Zane didn't flinch. He liked it.

Frosty vapors thickened and swirled around his calves like tentacles. They climbed higher up his thighs, torso, and to his shoulders. His skin prickled, and his nipples hardened from the chill. A sigh of pleasure slipped from his lips.

The pale mist deepened into a noxious shade of green and enveloped him. He couldn't see beyond it.

Something whispered in his ear.

"Zaaaane..."

The vapors dissipated, unveiling an alien landscape ripped from a nightmare. He was no longer in his shower. A mountainous horizon blazed with blue flames. The biting air seared his lungs.

The icy terrain was desolate, scattered with sharp rocks and gaping pits. Twisted trees reached up to the sky. Zane was shivering naked within a macabre painting, a cruel artist's depiction of Hell frozen over.

A woman descended from the clouds and appeared before him. Her eyes were icy blue like his, but colder. He'd seen them before—in the mirror at Snaxtime.

Her black hair spiraled around her like writhing serpents. She wore a gold bodice resembling skeletal bones, and a winged crown adorned with sapphires and crystals.

Demonika.

Her eyes glowed as she drifted closer. She extended her hand toward Zane.

"Come to me," she whispered, her voice soft as silk, wrapping itself around his mind.

Zane felt his legs weaken, his will slipping as her dark presence enveloped him, drawing him closer.

As he braced for the inevitable, a chant boomed across the hellscape. Zane turned toward the sound and gasped.

It was Hunter.

"*GLOTH URN ZOGH!*" Hunter repeated the foreign words again and again.

The young man's arms were outstretched. His skin was smooth as porcelain. He was chiseled like a god.

His commands disrupted the demon's advance. She hung in mid-air like she was stuck in a spiderweb.

"GLOTH URN ZOGH!"

Upon Hunter's final syllable, a high-pitched scream tore through the air. Everything shook. The woman's lips pulled back in a snarl before she was flung back into the horizon. Her scream faded into silence.

She was gone.

Hunter moved toward Zane. He reached out his hand and rested it gently on Zane's bare chest. A euphoric shockwave surged from Hunter's palm into Zane's core.

"Power awaken within," Hunter whispered.

Zane stiffened.

The shrill ring of Zane's alarm clock snapped him back to reality. His sheets were damp.

What just happened? It was all a dream. The details were already slipping away.

His phone pinged with a notification: BREAKING NEWS: SERIAL KILLER CLAIMS ANOTHER VICTIM AT PARADISE HOTEL

Zane read the grisly details—a mutilated body discovered in a hotel room, decapitated and partly eaten.

He texted the link to his friends: *Another murder.*

Star replied quickly: *WHAT??*

Dexter: *No way! Should we scope out the hotel? Maybe we'll find something. I'm off tonight. You?*

Zane: *Yeah, I'm off too.*

Star: *Ugh I gotta close up. You guys go without me.*

Dexter: *Bummer. Ok Zane let's do it.*

Star: *Be careful ok?*

Dexter: *For sure. Nothing risky. Quick in and out.*

Zane: *Let's meet at 8.*

The sun was setting as Dexter and Zane approached the Paradise Hotel. It was a tall historic building in a rough part of town.

Police barricades blocked the entrance, and officers were everywhere.

"This doesn't look good," Zane said.

Dexter eyed the scene. "I've got an idea. Follow my lead."

Dexter walked up to the barricade with authority. "Good evening, officers. We're here to... uh, help with the investigation," he improvised.

A skeptical officer looked at Dexter. "And you are?"

Dexter faltered for a moment. "We're... um, undercover investigators. I'm Special Agent Dimitri Volkov, and this is my colleague Special Agent Sven Jorgensen. They call him the Viking."

Zane nodded with a grunt.

"Oh yeah? And just what kind of investigators are you, Agent Volkov and — Viking?" the officer asked.

"We're with the Federal Anomalies Recon Team, the, uh, F-A-R-T," Dexter said, trying to keep a straight face as he realized what he had just spelled out. Zane swallowed a laugh as the other officers chuckled.

"*FART*, huh? That's a new one. I'm going to need to see some identification, boys," the officer responded.

Dexter fumbled in his pockets. "Uh, you know what? I think we left our official documentation in the car. Just give us a sec, BRB."

Dexter could hear the officers laughing at him as they retreated.

Once out of earshot, Zane exhaled. "Really, Dex? *FART?*"

"Yeah, well, it played out better in my head." Undeterred, Dexter gestured toward the rear of the building. "Let's try the back. There's gotta be another way in."

Overgrown weeds and trash blanketed the area behind the hotel. They searched for a way in, but their hopes faded with each locked door and sealed window.

"This sucks." Dexter kicked a wall.

"What sucks?"

"*I* suck," came his flat reply.

"Dude, why would you say that?"

Dexter looked up. "I just... I'm always failing at everything."

"No way!" Zane protested. "I could never do what you did back there. Sure, FART wasn't the best, but you were quick on your feet. That was badass! And I love my new nickname, the Viking."

"Whatever." Dexter looked down, deflecting the praise. "It feels like freshman year all over again."

"Freshman year?" Zane stepped toward Dexter and nudged him gently. "Hey, what's up?"

"High school wasn't easy for me," Dexter began. "Just a skinny kid with glasses, into pocket monster gaming and terrible at sports. Yeah, I wasn't setting the popularity charts on fire."

"Man, high school's not easy for anyone," Zane said.

Dexter sighed. "They had a field day with me — *Dexter the Dork*. I was a walking target. Every day was a nightmare, just trying to get through without being picked on or pushed around."

He took a beat. "The jokes and pranks, getting teased in gym class. I was always on edge, constantly reminded that I was a loser."

Zane knew pretty well what it felt like to be an outsider. He had never really been bullied, just invisible. He'd grown used to it, but seeing Dexter feel that way struck a chord with him.

Dexter scrunched his face. "The worst of 'em was Mike Henderson, the ringleader. He always had this smug smirk on his face. He totally got off on making my life miserable.

"This one time in the locker room," Dexter's voice cracked. "Mike and his goonies cornered me while I was changing and yelled, 'ATOMIC WEDGIE!' He hoisted me up in the air by my tighty-whities. The more I squirmed, the worse it got. They all cheered, and then Mike threw me out into the hallway, basically naked. All in front of a bunch of popular girls too. They all pointed and died laughing—I've never been more humiliated."

Zane clenched his fists. "That's messed up, man. I'm so sorry. Fuck Mike Henderson."

"Needless to say, I've since switched to boxer briefs." Dexter forced a smile. "You know, the whole 'class clown' thing started because of that. I figured out pretty quick that if I made people laugh, they'd like me more. And yes, I'm painfully aware that I'm a walking cliché."

"There's nothing cliché about you, Dex. You're one in a million. And you definitely know how to make *me* laugh."

Dexter smiled. "Actually, at my lowest, I met Jake. We were like this unexpected duo. He defended me more than once. Even though he's a total jock, he's got a heart of gold and really cares about his friends. He always laughs at my jokes—even the bad ones.

"He started pulling me into his videos, doing all sorts of goofy stuff. Next thing I know, people are noticing me, and

I'm getting followers. It gave me a boost when I needed it most. Made me feel like I belonged."

Zane nodded. "Yeah, he's good people."

"He got me the job at Snaxtime, too. Which was the best thing for me. It's sort of given me a purpose. Especially now, with all this demon investigation stuff. It sounds messed up, but it feels like I'm doing something important, something bigger than just making people laugh. Meeting you and Star, getting involved in all this... It's like I've found where I'm supposed to be."

"Sounds like everything led you to where you needed to be, even if it was a rough path. I sure get that."

"Yeah," Dexter said with a smirk. "All those wedgies must've started some weird butterfly effect that landed us all here. Fighting demons and saving the world. Go figure."

"I'm glad we're in this together." Zane smiled, his eyes glistening.

"I... I feel exactly the same way, my friend." Dexter agreed.

Zane tossed a rock. "Speaking of fighting demons and saving the world, I guess we're back to where we started. This was kind of a bust."

"Yeah, Star didn't miss out on much. There's no way into this hotel — not today, at least. Nothing to see here." Dexter looked around. "Nada."

Zane playfully hooked an arm around Dexter's neck and brought him closer, ruffling his hair with his other hand.

"Alright, kid, let's call it a night."

But their retreat was suddenly interrupted. Three men staggered toward them. They were drunk—and they smelled drunk too.

A burly guy with a scruffy beard and a torn leather jacket sneered at Dexter. "Well, well, what do we have here? A couple of sweethearts, how cute."

His two friends looked like trouble. One, tall and lanky with a mohawk, made kissing noises. The other, short and stocky, snickered as they closed in.

Dexter tried to step back, but the one with the mohawk blocked his path. "Hey, *nerd,* lost your way to the library?"

Zane stepped forward, his voice firm. "Back off, guys. We don't want any trouble."

Dexter, feeling emboldened by Zane's presence, couldn't resist a sarcastic retort. "Nice to see the local wildlife's thriving."

That did it. The scruffy guy got angry. He smashed his beer bottle against a wall and pressed the jagged edge to Dexter's neck. "You think you're funny, you little shit? I'll carve up that smug face of yours."

Dexter's bravado evaporated. He squirmed as the other two grabbed his arms.

Zane shouted, "Let him go!"

But the man pressed the glass harder against Dexter's jugular. "Aw, what are you gonna do about it?"

"GET OFF HIM!" Zane yelled. His voice echoed with an unexpected boom. A sudden energy coursed through his veins. He thrust his hands forward, and a torrent of power sent the punks flying in all directions.

Dexter remained standing. He was shaking, but unharmed. "Holy shit, Zane! Did you really just do that?!"

Zane looked down at his hands in disbelief as the men ran off. Tiny threads of electricity crackled in his palms before fading away. "Power awaken within."

"What did you say?" Dexter asked.

"I just remembered my dream from last night. Text Star—I have to fill you guys in."

The three friends met up at a donut shop after Star's shift.

"You did *what?!*" Star couldn't believe it.

Dexter was exuberant. He cozied up to Zane. "You shoulda seen this guy. He was unreal. It was like *Mortal Kombat.*" He brought a pink-frosted donut up to his heart and looked up at Zane. "My hero."

"I'm telling you guys," Zane said. "After that dream with Hunter and the demon... I don't know, it's like he unlocked something in me. When those guys attacked, it just... happened."

"And you think this Hunter guy from your dream gave you these... powers?" Star asked.

Dexter nodded vigorously. "It was incredible, Star! One minute we're cornered, the next, STRIKE—Zane's knocking 'em down like bowling pins!"

"It was crazy. I don't know what happened, but that dream felt totally real. The demon—Demonika—she felt so real. Hunter too."

"I told you that guy was super intense at Snaxtime yesterday. Maybe he just got into your head," Star said.

Zane looked down at his hands, still trying to make sense of it all. "Everything is connected. It has to be. The journal, the dream, the demon, the murders… this power… Hunter…" Zane realized he was rambling. He looked up at his friends.

Star remained skeptical. "So, you're, like, magical now?"

"I don't even know." Zane shrugged.

Dexter's eyes sparkled with excitement. "We should totally test it out! Let's see if you can do it again, Zane."

"Yeah, Wonder Boy, let's see this in action." Star finished off her iced coffee with a drawn-out slurp. "There's a playground right across the street. How 'bout we go and test out these magical superpowers you miraculously got from your dream crush?"

The old playground was deserted. Star had picked the right spot—there were lots of things to test Zane's so-called powers on.

"Monkey bars!" Dexter called out, skipping over to the structure. He jumped up and started swinging. The metal was rusted.

"I hope you've had your shots, Dexter," Star warned.

He let go of the bars and brushed his palms on his jeans. "Fortune favors the bold, my friend."

"Okay, how about that swing over there?" Star challenged Zane. "Make it move."

"I don't think it works that way," Zane stared at the swing. "But here goes nothing." He tried to tap into the mysterious energy he had felt earlier that night.

C'mon, move. Concentrate. Move.

The swing didn't move. He felt a tickle in his stomach, but it could have been the coffee and jelly donut he had just eaten.

He could feel Star's eyes burrowing into the back of his head.

Don't give up. You can't give up.

He locked his focus onto the swing. The plastic orange seat had a crack down the middle. Two weathered chains held it up.

Move.

The swing started to sway. It was subtle but noticeable.

"Am I doing this, or is it just the wind?" Zane asked.

Star squinted. "It's hard to tell, but it's definitely moving."

Dexter cheered, "Come on, Zane, you've got this!"

Encouraged, Zane took a deep breath and focused harder.

Suddenly, the fluttering in his stomach turned electric.

The swing's movement became more pronounced, creaking as it gained momentum.

"That's it!" Dexter shouted.

Star stepped closer. "If you're really doing this, make it stop and start again."

Zane nodded, his eyes never leaving the swing. He imagined it coming to a halt and channeled all his energy into stopping it. But the swing kept swaying.

The feeling in his core fizzled.

"Hmmph, must be the breeze after all," Star concluded.

"I can't do it," Zane muttered in defeat. "This is stupid."

"Don't give up. How bout we try something else?" Dexter pointed at the see-saw.

"Sure, but I really don't know what I'm doing here, guys," Zane said.

He moved over to the seesaw, wiped the sweat from his brow, and exhaled.

Hello, see-saw.

The wooden beam was splintered. He could almost feel every jagged edge.

Dexter watched with bated breath. "Come on, Zane. I believe in you, man!"

Star was getting impatient. "Ugh, let's quit while we're ahead, assuming we ever were."

Focus.

Minutes passed in silence. Zane closed his eyes.

Up… Down… Up… Down.

The see-saw moved slightly.

"YES!" Dexter's excitement was immediate. "Did you guys see that?"

"That was you, Zane?" Star's skepticism was waning.

Zane opened his eyes. "Did it move?"

"Yeah, but only like an inch," Star replied.

"That wasn't the wind this time!" Dexter yelled.

Motivated by this small success, Zane tried again. He closed his eyes and slipped back into the zone.

He felt it—his body charging with energy like a battery. Slowly, the see-saw moved again, tilting half a foot off the ground before falling back into place.

Dexter clapped his hands. "This is insane! You're actually doing it!"

Star was excited, too. "Try to make it go all the way."

Zane exhaled, visualizing the object moving by his will.

It tilted up until gravity took over and brought it down on the other side.

It was extraordinary.

"This is so awesome!" Dexter giggled like a little kid. He ran over to a bunny-shaped spring rider. "Zane, do this one!"

Zane stood in front of it and extended his hands.

Alright, rabbit, let's see what you can do.

The rabbit was made of metal and painted baby blue. It had chubby white cheeks and a red button nose.

It took a few minutes, but sure enough, it began to tremble.

"Oh my God." Star was finally a believer.

Zane's body buzzed with energy. The rabbit rocked back and forth with ease.

He was getting the hang of it, and the thrill of control was invigorating. Each breath deepened his connection to his environment as if he were tapping into a hidden energy grid.

He wanted more.

Hunter's strange words from the dream came to him. Before he knew it, he had said them out loud. *"Gloth urn zog."*

The bunny responded instantly. It rocked faster and faster.

"Whoa, Zane… Slow down there, buddy." Dexter's excitement dampened.

The metal bunny's motion grew violent. It slammed back and forth into the ground as though trying to put itself out of its misery.

Star grabbed Dexter's hand. "Um, Zane?"

With a startling crack, the bunny's head exploded.

"Zane!" Star yelled as one of its ears shot toward her. It grazed her pigtail as she jumped out of the way to dodge it.

"STAR! Are you okay?" Dexter ran over and hugged her.

She was in shock.

Zane dropped to his knees. His hands were shaking. "I don't know what happened. I can't control this..." *Whatever this is.*

Star came to. "Oh my God, that was, like, way too close. What happened?"

"I think I repeated what Hunter said in my dream. It just came out." Zane was confused. "I swear I didn't even know what I was saying."

"I'm okay," Star assured. "But, like, how about we stop with the weird chanting until we know what it means? And maybe we put the book back in the basement, just to be safe." She reached out her hand.

Zane pulled Snaxton's journal from his backpack and gave it to Star. Keeping it away from their homes seemed safest for now.

Zane lay in bed. The incident at the playground had shaken him. These powers, though exhilarating, were dangerous and uncontrollable.

And Hunter... Hunter was an enigma. The need to see him again, to get answers, was overwhelming.

Anxious, he clenched his fists. Prominent veins snaked along his forearms, glowing faintly beneath his skin and throbbing with his heartbeat. He flexed, noticing his muscles had become stronger and more defined.

He jumped out of bed and grabbed a pair of dumbbells. They were surprisingly light. He looked in the mirror. With each curl, his biceps bulged and grew bigger. He was a transformed version of himself, more sculpted and powerful. *Whoa.*

The window flew open with a gust of glittery pink mist. He walked over to it. The sky was a surreal canvas of purple velvet, with stars twinkling like emeralds and the moon shining like a giant diamond.

Everything was alive and intense, and connected to him in a way he couldn't explain. He closed the window and went back to bed.

Just as Zane's eyes shut, a tapping at the window jolted him awake. He clambered out of bed and stumbled over, his fingers opening the latch.

"Hunter?" Zane's voice quivered as he saw the figure perched outside.

A soft "Zane" floated through the air.

Hunter climbed into his bedroom. They sat down on the bed and faced each other.

"What are you doing here? Who are you?" Zane didn't know where to start. "What did you do to me? These… powers." He was desperate.

"You will understand in time." Hunter tilted his head. "I did not give you these powers. I helped you find them."

Zane's confusion deepened. "How? What? I'm really scared."

"I will guide you, teach you. You have a great power within, Zane. You are special."

"Okay, teach me now," Zane sat up straight. "Where do we start?"

"Soon," Hunter replied. "But I must go now."

Zane's mind raced. "You can't go!"

"I am sorry."

"Tell me who you are. Is this really happening? Are you really here?" Zane realized this might be another dream. "Wait, if this *is* real, meet me at the carnival tomorrow night."

"I am real."

"Then meet me at the carnival! At eight."

"I will be there."

Zane grabbed Hunter's thigh. "Please, stay."

Hunter placed his hand on Zane's. Their eyes locked. A connection was charging between them. Zane felt complete at that moment.

Hunter moved his lips closer to Zane's, grazing them as he whispered, "Wake up."

Zane's eyes opened to the light of morning. *Hunter.* He was alone.

He lay there for a moment, trying to distinguish dream from reality. The only way to know for sure would be at the carnival.

Tonight, he would get answers.

CHAPTER EIGHT

J ake scrubbed the counter until the only thing left behind was his reflection. Marjorie had asked him to work late and close up last minute, but he didn't mind. He was actually kind of stoked, thinking about the doggie selfie stick he wanted to buy for Biscuits' Instagram.

With his pods in his ears, he grabbed a mop and started dancing around the tables and chairs. The upbeat music made the chore way less boring. He swayed and shuffled his feet to the beat, turning mopping into a fun little dance.

It couldn't hurt to get this on video. Despite the nightmare of the sauce incident, he hadn't been totally canceled. Even though he'd been the face of probably one of the worst product launches ever, his more forgiving fans still adored him. And now, he was finally starting to gain followers again. Sure, dancing with a mop might look goofy, but they would love it. He could already hear the notifications rolling in.

Jake propped the mop against a table and grabbed his phone. He flipped open the camera and checked himself out. He knew he looked good—no shame in that. He modeled for his phone, pouting his lips and throwing in a wink for good measure.

He looked around for the best spot to set up. The counter by the cash register was the right height and gave a good view of the dining area for his dance. He placed his phone against the register and made sure the angle was perfect.

Jake pressed record. He held the mop handle close to him, transforming it into his dance partner. They swayed together across the floor in perfect harmony. The mop spun under his touch as if they had practiced together for hours.

Mid-routine, he flexed his bicep, then playfully lifted his shirt to reveal his impressive six-pack. He glided across the shining tiles, then leaped, twirled, and pirouetted. It was quite the performance.

He stopped the recording. For sure, this one would get a lot of likes. When he reviewed the video, he noticed something scurrying behind him during his dance. He yanked out his pods and scanned the room. Nothing. He returned to his screen and looked at the paused video. Whatever had moved past him was a blurry shape, probably one of the rats causing trouble lately. Although, judging by the size, that would have to be one giant rat! He shook it off, made some quick edits, and posted the clip.

His phone started to vibrate as the notifications poured in. Feeling validated, Jake put his phone down, grabbed two garbage bags, and headed to the dumpster behind the restaurant.

He lifted the first bag with a grunt and swung it into the open container. It landed with a hollow thud. From inside the dumpster, something began to rustle.

His mind, trying to find a rational explanation, defaulted to the usual culprit—rats. The area behind Snaxtime had its share of nocturnal scavengers. He dismissed it as a typical occurrence. With a second attempt at bravado, he hoisted the next bag and tossed it into the dumpster.

The bag landed with another clunk, and then... silence. But the silence was short-lived. A guttural growl emanated from the bin's depths.

This was no rat.

Jake broke out in goosebumps. He gave the dumpster a good kick.

The growling stopped. Jake stood frozen with his eyes locked on the dumpster. Every little sound seemed louder—the steady drip from a leaky pipe, a distant car alarm, even his own breath.

Several heart-thumping moments passed, but the sound didn't happen again. Jake headed back inside.

He paused mid-step, just shy of the restaurant door, when something giggled behind him.

Panicked, he willed his body to turn around.

A tiny creature stood in front of the dumpster on two clawed feet. Its sickly green skin was covered in slimy goo. Bald and nasty-looking, its face was dominated by sharp, mangled teeth. Green drool oozed from its mouth.

The critter clutched a chicken nugget in its claws, munching away on its crispy prize. Jake gasped, and the creature looked up. It dropped the nugget, its beady eyes locking onto Jake. It hissed and started prowling toward him like a cat on the hunt.

Jake's body flooded with adrenaline as he bolted back into the restaurant and rammed the door shut. The door shook with aggressive thuds and frenzied clawing from the other side.

He pushed a table in front of the door. The pounding stopped. He was sweating and shaking. As he backed away, he tripped on the mop and bucket, spilling soapy water onto the floor.

Jake steadied himself. He stood as still as he could.

Then he heard it—a sound, more like a melody. It was seductive and gentle, stirring something inside Jake. He followed the song into the kitchen. It was coming from the walk-in freezer.

Fear told him to run and hide behind the counter. But the music pulled him in. His legs felt like they were made of cement, moving on their own. Each step closer to the freezer felt like trudging through thick molasses.

He reached for the freezer door, but it opened on its own.

An intoxicating aroma wafted out—the smell of temptation. He went deeper into the icy chamber.

The door slammed shut behind him. The sudden jolt of reality hit him hard and broke his trance.

He shoved against the door, but it was locked. He was trapped.

Cold seeped through his clothes and nipped at his skin. His teeth chattered.

He pounded at the door with his fists. It didn't budge. His physical strength wouldn't save him.

It was pitch black.

Out of nowhere, cold fingers sneaked under his shirt and climbed up his torso. They traced patterns on his skin as they journeyed across his smooth chest. His muscles tensed.

The hands didn't stop. They glided up to his shoulders and then down to his quivering biceps. The sensation was unfamiliar but electrifying—like ice sparking with heat. He was getting aroused.

Just as he started to lose himself, a woman's voice grazed his ear.

"Jaaaake…"

A startling realization dawned upon him. He was in danger.

A sudden heat, like a dragon's breath, seared his neck. His fear intensified, suffocating his bravery and twisting his mind.

He sliced his arms through the air in wild arcs. But there was nothing there.

The invisible hands that had been caressing his skin suddenly attacked. Sharp claws shredded through his shirt, leaving burning trails on his flesh.

The pain was unbearable. His hands floundered to fend off the force, only to land on his own skin, slick and wet with blood. The metallic tang of it seeped into his nostrils. He could hear his blood splattering onto the floor.

Two glowing eyes came out of nowhere.

Jake wailed. But his cry was smothered.

The restaurant was quiet except for the pinging of Jake's phone, amassing likes on what would be his final post.

CHAPTER NINE

Zane skated through the streets as the Ferris wheel came into view. His mind was adrift. Ever since that night he almost kissed Star at the lake, he had wondered if she really liked him. Yet with the demon threat looming, romance had slid to the backburner.

Still, he couldn't deny there was a connection. Or could he? Because now there was Hunter.

How was it possible Zane felt so consumed by someone he barely knew? What strange spell made it impossible to concentrate whenever Hunter invaded his thoughts? In comparison, his feelings for Star seemed juvenile, like a middle school crush.

Hunter ignited an obsessive flame, and Zane hardly recognized himself anymore. *Am I falling in love?*

All Zane knew was he needed to see Hunter again tonight.

And just like that, he was there.

Hunter glowed under the carnival lights. He was dressed head to toe in black, with a shiny satin bomber jacket, jeans, and boots.

"You came." Zane blushed. *It wasn't just a dream.*

"Hello, Zane. I am glad you are here." He looked so beautiful.

"I need… I need to know… Who are you?"

"Come with me," Hunter beckoned, leading Zane into the crowd. "I have never been to one of these before," he confessed, his eyes roaming over the bustling scene.

Zane raised an eyebrow. "Seriously? A carnival virgin?"

Hunter smiled. "There are a lot of things I have never done."

Zane grabbed Hunter's arm and steered him off to a quiet spot behind the Tilt-a-Whirl. He turned to face Hunter. "Alright, man, no more secrets. Who are you, *really?* And what's going on?"

"I will tell you everything, Zane. But it is a long story."

"I've got all night."

"Then I will begin." Hunter sat on a bench, and Zane joined him. "It all started 300 years ago, when Paradise Falls was just a small village. There was a rash of murders. Men were slaughtered, their bodies found in pieces."

"Just like what's been happening here, now," Zane said.

"Yes."

"So what happened?"

"The villagers did not believe a human could have done such things—tearing men apart like prey. It had to be something wild, something dangerous. They searched the forest for the animals responsible, but the culprit remained a mystery.

"The deaths mounted for months. Eventually, a hunting party found a cave deep in the woods. In it lived a demon queen. She was a seductress, a succubus with an insatiable hunger for men. She consumed their souls to feed her power."

Zane was captivated. "Demonika."

"Yes."

"What did they do to her?"

"She was too powerful to kill. In their desperation to stop her, the village leaders turned to powerful sorcery. Through an arcane ritual, they managed to entomb her…"

The sudden intrusion of four rowdy teens shattered the moment. They stumbled toward Zane and Hunter, laughing and stinking of weed and tequila.

One of them, a kid in a backward baseball cap, held out a joint. "Hey, bros, wanna puff?"

Hunter looked confused. Zane stood up. "Nah, dude, we're all set, thanks." He pulled Hunter off the bench and pointed to a nearby ride. "Let's check that out."

They approached the Tunnel of Love, where a swan-shaped boat awaited them. "What kind of ride is this?"

Hunter asked as they sat down. Soft rock music drifted out from the heart-shaped entrance in front of them.

"Let's just say it'll be quiet in here," Zane said, almost apologetically.

As their boat floated away from prying eyes and ears into the pink tunnel, Zane prodded for more. "So, what happened after they put Demonika in the tomb?"

"A clandestine order arose, dedicated to keeping the village safe from the demon's influence forever. They designed a powerful weapon against her—a spell they would pass down through their descendants, giving their bloodline the power to banish her should she ever escape again."

"And she has escaped! So, we just need to find a *descendant*." Zane was finally getting answers.

Hunter warned that a descendant's power could also be used to permanently resurrect the demon. "A dark sect formed alongside the order. They believed in Demonika's supremacy and wanted to release her. They targeted descendants for their plan, using deceit and cunning to hide their true intentions."

"So, we need to find a descendant before they do."

"The village elders were determined to prevent the dark sect from succeeding. They created a guardian by carving him from the tomb's rock," Hunter explained. "This guardian would watch over Demonika. If she ever escaped again, the statue would come to life and find a descendant who could reseal her."

Zane was struggling to keep up. "Okay, so we need to find a *guardian,* so they can find a *descendant* to banish the demon back to her tomb. Got it. Now, how do we find this guardian?"

"We do not need to find him," Hunter rested his hand on Zane's shoulder. "Because I have found you."

"Wait, what?"

"*I* am that guardian. And you, Zane Hawthorn... *You* are the last descendant."

Zane was reeling. Then, his mind went completely blank. He saw the dreamy scenery unfolding around them in the tunnel—an artificial moon, rose-draped trellises, and a fairy-tale castle painted in the distance. But as the ride's music swelled, Hunter's revelation came back into view.

Hunter's voice remained steady, "The ritual spell you and your friends conducted at Snaxtime... It broke the chains binding Demonika. You released her."

The guilt stung.

"This was not your doing, Zane," Hunter was quick to comfort him.

"But you just said I released her."

"Ancient forces were at play. You were marked by this magic long before you knew it. It was always going to find you."

Zane scoffed, "Well, it found me."

Hunter continued, "And now I have found you. Demonika's escape led to my awakening. I ventured forth to seek you, to mentor you, and to guide you toward your destiny."

It was a hard reality to swallow, but Zane knew deep down that Hunter's words held truth.

It's my destiny.

The Tunnel of Love's journey ended.

"Well, that was romantic," Zane joked.

They moved to the Ferris wheel. As they ascended into the night sky, the world below shrank away.

"This demon has been freed only once before, decades ago." The carriage swayed as Hunter continued his tale.

"We read about that in the library. In the '70s?"

"Yes, she was summoned," Hunter said.

"Who would do that?"

"It was… Harold Snaxton."

"WHAT?!" The puzzle pieces started falling into place. "His journal…"

"Harold's lineage has been entwined with the dark sect for generations. His journal was his obsession. It chronicled extensive research, spells, and his experiments with the supernatural. The collected knowledge imbued the journal with a unique power. He devoted his entire life to resurrecting Demonika permanently."

"But someone stopped him?"

"Your great-uncle. He was the last descendant before you."

"Uncle *Reginald?!*"

"And he was not alone—many, including myself, rallied to his side to banish her."

"Was my father there? Did you know him, too?"

"Your father was very young then. Just a boy. He looked much like you, Zane."

"Do you know what happened to him? To my parents?"

"I do not. I never knew them in adulthood. My duty has kept me bound to the tomb, watching over Demonika. But this much is certain—you are the last of your line."

"So, let me get this straight. You're seriously telling me that I'm the end-of-the-line for some ancient, demon-battling sorcerers, and it's my destiny to give a demon lady the boot back to Hell, or we're all toast?" Zane was joking, but he wasn't smiling. "This *can't* be real. This is a dream, right?"

"Evil is rising, Zane."

"This is... It's a lot." Zane took a moment.

Hunter reached out. "I am here for you. I will train you and teach you about your powers. We will start tonight."

You can handle this.

Zane exhaled. "Okay, let's do it."

When their carriage touched down, he looked at Hunter and smiled. "Wait, so you've really never been to a carnival?"

Hunter shrugged sheepishly.

"Dude, before we start training, I've got a few things to teach *you*."

Zane was eager to share the carnival's joys with Hunter. They walked toward a row of food trucks. Zane ordered two corn dogs. "Let's start with this," he said, pumping ribbons of mustard onto them.

Hunter examined the fried dog with fascination and took a bite. His eyes lit up. "Mmm, this is... incredible!" he marveled. Mustard was smudged at the corner of his lips.

"*Totally* incredible," Zane giggled.

"Yes, *totally* incredible," Hunter concurred.

"You should try cotton candy next," Zane said while buying a stick at the next stand. He passed the pink fluff to Hunter, who took a curious nibble. The sugary strands melted instantly on his tongue. "It is peculiarly delightful," Hunter noted with a look of surprise.

As they walked, Zane noticed the childlike wonder in Hunter's eyes. There was something touching about watching him indulge in the carnival's uncomplicated fun.

Their path led them to a Test-Your-Strength game. A beefy guy covered in tattoos gripped the mallet, muscles bulging, and swung with all his might. The puck shot up, ringing the bell loudly. The crowd cheered.

Zane, impressed, nudged Hunter playfully. "Think you can top that?" he teased.

Hunter eyed the game with amusement. "I will give it a try." He approached the game and grasped the mallet. He swung with ease. The puck didn't just ring the bell — it broke through the top, sending it flying into the air and clattering to the ground several feet away.

The crowd erupted into applause and cheers. Zane's mouth hung open in disbelief. "How did you...?"

Hunter winked, handing the mallet back to the stunned carny, who presented him with a giant stuffed monkey wearing sunglasses as his prize.

"You're a natural," Zane said, impressed. Hunter was stronger than he looked.

They moved on to the apple fritters truck. The aroma of sweet cinnamon and fried dough was intoxicating.

"And now for the main event," Zane said, ordering a batch of fritters and two jumbo grape slushies. The vendor handed them a bag of the golden, sugar-dusted delights, along with giant cups of frozen purple drink.

Hunter popped one into his mouth whole. He closed his eyes in bliss as he chewed. "This is... the best."

"Epic, right?"

Hunter ate another one. "*Totally* epic," he said with his mouth full.

Zane smiled. "You know... I sorta remember coming to a carnival like this with my parents. It's one of my only memories of them."

Hunter's eyes softened. "A happy memory."

"Yeah, for sure. I mostly remember the food. I think that's why I love these fritters so much. It's a faint memory, but it's there." Zane was feeling nostalgic. "Do you have any memories like that?"

The cheerfulness in Hunter's expression faded. "My past is... complicated."

Zane sensed the shift in Hunter's mood. "Oh yeah, sorry, I… wasn't thinking. But hey, it's all good. I mean, you're the coolest person I ever met. And you've changed my life forever. I'll never forget that."

A smile returned to Hunter's face. "I did not change your life. This was always your destiny. But I am happy to be a part of it. My time with you is a memory I will always cherish."

Zane raised his jumbo cup, "To many more memories together."

Hunter kept smiling as he sipped on his slushie, but there was melancholy in his eyes.

The sweetness of the moment mingled with the treats in their hands.

"We need to get started." Hunter guided Zane to a secluded spot behind the Ferris wheel. "You have a natural ability, like at the playground. I was watching you," he revealed.

"You saw me?" Zane was surprised.

"I've been... observing, waiting…"

"Waiting for what?"

"For you to discover your power on your own. Now I can teach you how to use it." Hunter took Zane's hands. "Focus on your hands, they are your primary tools for channeling energy."

He pointed to an overflowing recycling bin. "Let's start with something simple. Try moving one of those cans. Visualize the energy starting from your chest. Let it move into your arms and out through your fingertips."

Zane held out his hands and zeroed in on a soda can. Aiming to recreate the energy burst he felt at the playground, he focused with all his might. A tingling sensation began in his chest, radiated into his arms, and out to his fingers.

The can wobbled and then rolled off the stack of garbage.

"There, you see?" Hunter reassured. "You are manipulating physical objects using your energy. Now move it from the ground and place it right side up on that table over there."

Zane's fingertips still buzzed, feeling charged. He confidently stared down the can.

"Focus," Hunter encouraged.

Zane envisioned energy beams linking his fingers and the can. To his shock, it actually began to hover.

"Good, keep it steady," Hunter said.

The can sailed through the air and settled on the table.

"I did it!"

"You are on the right track, Zane. But remember, without control, your gift can become unpredictable."

"It's about precision," Zane said.

"Precisely," Hunter replied. "Power is a responsibility. You are learning quickly, but remember to always stay mindful of your strength and its potential consequences."

Loud music blared from the nearby bumper cars as Hunter pointed to the stuffed monkey he had won, now resting on a bench. "Let's try something different. Make the animal dance."

Zane eyed the plush toy, its oversized limbs hanging comically. He focused on the heavy bass, picturing the monkey swaying to the rhythm. Extending his hands, he tried to will it to move. The monkey quivered but stayed motionless.

"Okay, Zane, try using your voice. Sometimes, a verbal command can help focus your intention."

Zane directed his attention to the toy. "Dance."

The monkey twitched, then began to jerk erratically.

"Again," Hunter encouraged.

"DANCE!" Zane demanded with authority. The stuffed animal responded by flailing. It thrashed without any rhythm. Zane's frustration mounted.

"Control it, Zane. Let the beat guide you," Hunter instructed as the music thumped in the background.

Zane's hands trembled with energy. He needed to make it work. Without thinking, the words came out of him, as if from somewhere deep inside—"*GLOTH URN ZOG!*"

The monkey exploded in a violent burst, scattering its remains in a snowstorm of stuffing. Zane stumbled back, his breath ragged, staring at the shredded pieces in shock.

"I—I didn't mean to," Zane stammered. "The words... they just came out."

"Do you know what you just said?" Hunter looked serious.

Zane shook his head. "No. It just... happened."

"That was Zoghrul," Hunter said. "An ancient language, powerful beyond measure. It amplifies magic and makes spells stronger. But if you do not know how to control it, it can be dangerous. *Very* dangerous."

"Zoghrul? I didn't even realize I was saying anything. It was like at the playground, when the bunny exploded."

"Yes, exactly like at the playground," Hunter said. "The same words, the same result."

"You said those words against Demonika in my dream… What do they mean?" Zane asked.

"There is no direct translation. The spell I used, and you echoed, can repel or even banish evil. But Zoghrul is not just a language. It is raw power. And if you do not know what the words mean or how to control them..."

"So what do I do?" Zane interrupted.

"Right now, you have to focus on controlling your energy—using your hands and your voice with precision. With practice, you will get there. But until then, do not use Zoghrul. Do you understand?"

"Yeah... I understand." Zane looked at the destroyed monkey and realized just how dangerous his power could be. "I'll do better."

Hunter nodded. "Now, let's keep going. There is more to learn."

As Zane's training grew more intense, he found himself manipulating objects with growing ease using his hands. However, mastering voice commands remained a challenge.

His confidence was building, along with his attachment to Hunter. Zane didn't want the night to end. Nobody had ever cared for him like this. He remembered then how Hunter had left him in his dream. Everyone had always left him.

He hated the idea of being alone again.

It was getting late, but there was still time left for a little fun before the carnival closed. Zane scanned the horizon and spotted a neon-lit funhouse called The Hellhole. Tombstones tilted near the entrance and plastic skeletons dangled from chains. Exaggerated killer clowns with crazed smiles leered behind barred windows. The building was striped in zig-zags.

Zane snatched Hunter's hand. "Have you ever been in a funhouse?" Before Hunter could respond, Zane pulled him toward the beckoning gates of The Hellhole.

Hunter hesitated as they crossed the threshold. "Wait…"

But it was too late. Zane had already stepped inside, and Hunter had disappeared.

"Hunter?"

Zane stood alone in an entry hall. He squinted as his eyes adjusted to the dim room. It was decorated like a classic haunted house—candelabras flickered, cobwebs sprawled in the corners, and wallpaper crumbled off the walls.

But where was Hunter? Zane turned and opened the door to the outside again, but nobody was there.

He froze as he heard Hunter's voice calling for him from somewhere inside.

What's happening?

Before him, three doors vied for his attention. One bore a cherub, its hands pressed together in worship. Another was swathed in chains and padlocks. And the third door was covered in thorny vines. Zane reached for the door with the angel.

He stepped into a chapel that was anything but holy. A red neon cross hung defiantly upside down. The distant strains of grim organ music played.

"Hunter?"

Beneath the cross was an altar, where a chalice filled with blood cascaded its contents like a fountain. Black candles surrounded the altar and lined the walls. Stained-glass windows depicted horrifying scenes of Hell.

But it was the lone figure in the front pew that caught Zane's attention. A nun in traditional habit kneeled in prayer. As Zane approached, she spun around in a jarring, mechanical motion, revealing a skeletal face. An earsplitting shriek and a sudden puff of stale air accompanied the movement. He thought to himself how impressive the props and special effects were for a run-of-the-mill local carnival. While Zane loved a good haunted house, his focus remained undeterred from finding Hunter.

To his left, a door swung open with a loud creak. It was a confessional booth, spewing forth a plume of smoke. Zane entered.

He felt claustrophobic in the dark booth. From behind the latticed grille, two red eyes glared at him, while whispers recited a corrupted Hail Mary, overlaid with labored breathing. Searching the booth, he found that the wall beside him concealed a small door. He pushed it open and crawled through.

Zane ventured into a new room—a hall of mirrors. The door sprung shut, incarcerating him within a web of warped reflections. Distorted circus music blared.

Zane ambled in the dizzying labyrinth, his own reflection twisted and elongated in the reflective glass.

"HUNTER!"

Hunter's image fanned out across multiple glass panels. Zane chased the elusive apparition, his desperation intensifying as it continued to split and multiply, always just out of reach.

Finally, he stumbled into a stretched-out corridor. At the end of the hallway was a black door, framed in strips of pink light. Green mist oozed out from underneath.

A female voice sang out his name, "Zaaaane…"

The fog grew denser. When he opened the door, he was instantly thrown into the same demon world from his dream.

The red sky was marred by black clouds. The ground undulated beneath him, as if alive. The pungent scent of sulfur assaulted his nostrils.

And there she was, the bewitching phantom from his nightmare. Zane was gripped by panic. There was no visible escape. The siren's song grew louder, anchoring itself deeper, and rooting him to the spot. The whites of his eyes turned black.

Demonika's smile broadened unnaturally across her face. "Join me," her voice echoed. "Together, we will make my return complete. I shall rule forevermore. Ghouls rise, heed my song!" She flew into the air and began chanting in Zoghrul.

"TUROG, SKRAB, KLIVO NIHZ DRON!"

Her aria stirred the mist into a storm around her. The ground beneath Zane convulsed. Scores of tiny, sharp claws erupted from the trembling soil, revealing an army of diminutive green creatures. They spewed out of the earth and congregated at the feet of the demon. Their misshapen forms created a writhing mountain of flesh.

Ensnared by her voice, Zane was drawn toward the floating figure. He started his treacherous ascent up the heaving mound of squirming monsters.

Her fingers curled, summoning him closer. When Zane reached the demon, he dropped to his knees. She wrapped him in a tight, unyielding embrace.

Suddenly, a powerful force tore Zane from Demonika's grip, hurling him backward. A blinding light exploded, swallowing everything in white.

Zane's eyes blinked open.

"You are safe here," Hunter whispered. Zane was cradled in his arms.

He was in a world utterly different from anything he'd seen before. Candy-colored clouds, pink and blue, hung in an airbrushed sky.

Surrounding him, crystal formations jutted from the ground, their glittering bodies defying any sense of earthly gravity.

Zane noticed Hunter had transformed into a vision of celestial splendor. His flawless and smooth skin resembled pure marble, and his hair sparkled like silver. He was draped in a green cape, which he opened to expose an emerald jewel set within his sculpted chest.

The gemstone, cut into the shape of an eye, pulsed with light like a heartbeat. "This is my watchful eye." He drew Zane's fingers to the stone with a gentle guiding hand. It flared to life upon contact, swelling and bathing them in light.

"Whoa." Zane felt euphoric.

"It led me to you."

As Zane withdrew his hand, the stone's light dimmed. "So what do we do next?"

"Demonika's tomb is directly beneath Snaxtime," Hunter revealed. "You must unlock the banishing spell hidden within the journal and perform the ritual during the next full-blood lunar eclipse. But beware, in the wrong hands, this spell can amplify her powers, making her invincible."

Zane's heart raced. "What? How long do I have?" he asked, desperation creeping in.

"The eclipse is tomorrow night, at midnight."

Zane's voice wavered. "You'll be with me, right? Will you help me? Help me find the spell and do the ritual? I need you."

Hunter sighed. "My presence in the earthly realm takes a tremendous amount of energy. If I use too much now, I will not be there when you need me most.

"I will guide you, Zane, but I cannot be there every step of the way. You need to face this challenge on your own. It is the only way you'll grow stronger and become who you are meant to be."

Zane's heart sank. "But... What if I can't do it without you?"

"When the time comes, I will give myself to you. I will give you all the strength you need, even if it means giving up everything I have. I believe in you, Zane. But you must believe in yourself. This journey is yours to complete."

Zane nodded, though doubt still tugged at him.

Hunter continued, "Remember, I am always with you, even when you cannot see me. But this fight... It has to be yours. You will know the way. Trust that."

A million questions flooded Zane's mind, but before he could voice any of them, Hunter's emerald burst with light.

Zane was startled to find himself alone on top of the Ferris wheel.

He looked out at the city skyline as the ride descended. He could see Snaxtime nestled on a distant hill. An unsettling gloom appeared to shroud it.

Tonight, Zane had discovered that his fate was irrevocably entwined with a realm of magic and a secret world previously unknown to him.

His mission was clear: rally his friends, unearth the banishing spell, and wield his ancestral powers to send the demon queen back to her underground prison.

CHAPTER TEN

Zane sent a text to Star and Dexter: *Meet at Snaxtime ASAP.*

He was winded by the time he got there. Zane knew he was inviting his friends into danger. But he needed their help. They were stronger together.

Star's car screeched into the lot. She and Dexter burst out.

"Look…" Dexter pointed to a blue truck parked toward the back. "Is that Jake's? Is he still here this late?"

"That's weird." Zane hadn't even noticed Jake's truck. The restaurant looked dark and empty. "Doesn't look like he's inside."

Star dismissed the concern. "Someone probably picked him up to go party. He does it all the time."

"So, what's going on, Zane? Why are we here?" Dexter asked.

"There's so much to fill you in on." Zane brushed back his hair. His bicep was noticeably larger.

"Dang, hottie, have you been working out?" Star grabbed his arm.

"Yeah, sort of..." Zane looked down at himself. "I've been... training." He dove into his story. He detailed his encounter with Demonika and everything Hunter had revealed. It was a lot to digest, but Star and Dexter listened without interruption.

"That's like, totally unbelievable, Zane! But we're with you, right Dex?" Star turned to Dexter.

Dexter saluted, "Demon Patrol, reporting for duty!"

"We have to find that banishing spell," Zane pressed. "It's the only way to stop her. It's somewhere in the journal. I figured we could meet here and look for it together."

Dexter shrugged. "So, what are we waiting for?"

The trio entered Snaxtime.

Zane flipped the light switch, but nothing happened. "No power."

They pulled out their phones to light the way toward the basement.

"Ahhh!" Dexter stepped into a puddle of soapy water and slipped. Star and Zane heard the thud of his fall.

"Dexter!" Star's voice rang out. "You okay?!"

"Ouch!" Dexter grunted, embarrassed. He saw an overturned bucket next to him.

"Careful, Dex." Zane offered a hand and pulled him up.

Dexter picked up the bucket. "Strange, Jake would never leave a mess like this." He called out, "Yo, Jake!"

There was no response.

They went down to the basement. Star made a beeline for a box tucked away in a corner where she had safeguarded the journal.

They rifled through the book's pages. The journal was a patchwork of the extraordinary. Harold Snaxton's notes were in both English and what they now knew to be Zoghrul. The ancient language was frustratingly cryptic, and they could not make heads or tails of it. This made the task of finding the banishing spell nearly impossible.

"There must be a way to translate this," Star said.

Dexter let out a laugh, "Yeah, I don't think Google Translate knows *Zoghrul*."

Something in the book caught Zane's attention—an illustration of a jewel that looked just like Hunter's emerald eye. But before he could say anything, a crash from upstairs startled them.

"What was that?" Star whispered in fear. Zane tucked the journal into his backpack, and they snuck up the stairs to investigate.

They entered the kitchen. Zane crouched down and inspected underneath the counters. "Check this out." There were claw marks in the stainless steel.

Star looked at the marks. "Yikes, you think this is our demon lady's handiwork? Someone needs to introduce her to a manicurist."

Dexter gulped. "And maybe a priest."

Star noticed the supply closet door was ajar. She approached it with trepidation and pushed it open. "Oh my God... blood!" she gasped at the sight of a large, crimson pool on the ground.

Dexter hurried over. "Dude, that's not blood." He tasted a bit. "It's ketchup." Dexter knew his condiments, even in low light. The closet floor was littered with broken ketchup bottles and other sauces. Chewed-up food cartons were everywhere.

Star felt sick. She shut the closet door and wiped her jeans, trying to get rid of the gross feeling. "Ew, YUCK!" She gagged.

"Shhhh!" Dexter scolded. He saw something strange by the walk-in freezer. A crate was slathered in gooey green slime that was oozing onto the floor and collecting into a growing puddle. "Ummm... You gotta see this…" Dexter's voice cracked.

He pointed his flashlight at the green slime. "What do you think it is? Definitely not relish." He touched it, but his finger sizzled on contact. He jerked back in pain, howling and clutching his injured finger.

Maniacal giggles came from behind the crate. The unsettling snickers were followed by the pitter-patter of tiny scurrying feet. Quick movements swept around them.

Another crash came from inside the walk-in freezer.

Star grabbed a meat cleaver. Dexter picked up a heavy skillet. Zane, feeling his powers, flexed his hands open. They huddled together and edged toward the freezer door.

Zane reached for the handle, his other hand open and ready, as if drawing strength from the air itself. The door groaned open, releasing a blast of putrid air.

And then they saw something horrendous—a revolting parody of their friend, Jake. Part of his face was torn away, revealing a gruesome mask of bone, flesh, and sinew. His remaining features twisted into an unrecognizable grimace. One arm, its skin flayed, hung lifelessly by his side.

A grisly cavity marked where his heart used to beat. His brains seeped from the ravaged side of his skull.

Despite the horrific injuries, Jake moved. His steps were disjointed.

Star let out a bloodcurdling scream as Jake's mutilated corpse staggered toward her. Before the cry could fully escape, he wrapped his ragged fingers around her delicate neck in a vise grip.

Her face turned purple as he tightened his hold. Her bulging eyes pleaded for mercy but met only the soulless void in Jake's stare. The last wisps of air wheezed through her closing windpipe as he drew her toward his gnashing jaws.

She clutched the cleaver. With one forceful swing, she embedded the sharp blade into Jake's neck. He released his grip as blood sprayed everywhere like a sprinkler, painting her body and face glossy red. Jake's head flopped to the side, but the undead body pressed on.

Dexter swung the skillet against Jake's outstretched arm with a loud clang. The impact spun Jake around, sending him stumbling toward Dexter.

The zombie lunged at him. Dexter froze against the wall in fear.

Zane reached out toward an ice pick on a distant counter. With a flick of his magical fingers, the pick flew into his hand. He hurled it at Jake, striking him right between the eyes.

Jake swayed momentarily before crumpling to the ground.

Star's knuckles were bone-white on the steering wheel.

Dexter shuddered in the back seat. "Oh God, oh God, his guts... His guts were like falling out!"

Zane gripped his seat. "We just left him there... We just left him..."

"How could that be Jake? He was trying to kill us." Star sucked in a quavering breath.

"That wasn't Jake. Jake is dead," Zane said.

They drove aimlessly for hours. The sobering reality of Jake's fate was sinking in. His sunny presence was now a mere memory.

"Remember that day," Star began, her voice choked with

emotion, "when Jake talked in a fake British accent for the entire shift? It was so annoying. But he, like, totally pulled it off."

"With that perfect smile." Tears pooled in Dexter's eyes.

Zane clenched his jaw. *Damn this succubus to Hell.*

"We should go to the police. We need to report this," Dexter said.

"Seriously? We've already been through this. There's no time—they'd just hold us up." Star pulled over. She turned to the others. "Okay, this ends now. We need somewhere quiet to dig into this journal, unlock that spell, and banish this bitch."

Dexter wiped his cheek. "Where should we go?"

Star pulled back onto the street. "My house. No one's home except for my grandmother, and maybe we can try to talk to her, too." She looked down at her bloodstained clothes. "Besides, I totally need a shower. I'm basically Carrie at prom."

Emberheart Manor, Star's family home, was a mansion surrounded by well-kept lawns. It was clear the house was old. The paint was faded, and the detailed architecture was worn. Still, it was a grand estate.

They pulled into the driveway. Zane had never been to a house like this. "Whoa, Star. When were you planning on telling me you're secretly a princess?"

Dexter ribbed, "She prefers *Your Highness.*"

"Technically I'm more of a 'Lady' than 'her Royal Highness...' Lady Starling Rose Emberheart, pleased to make your acquaintance."

"Well, excuse me, *m'lady*," Dexter replied.

Star raised her nose snootily, feigning sophistication. "You can leave your horses by the stables. And gentlemen, please refrain from touching the artwork. Replicas are available in the gift shop."

They had spent the rest of the drive mourning in silence, so this moment of lightheartedness felt like a much-needed balm. Joking around was their way of coping with the horrific loss of one of their closest friends.

"Starling, huh? That's a pretty name," Zane said.

"I like Star better. Stars sparkle, like me." She winked.

"I like Star, too." Zane looked at the mansion. "Wow, this place is so cool."

"You should see the gardens." Dexter wiggled his eyebrows. "They've got every type of plant you can think of, and old statues. If you ask me, it's almost how I envision Konoha from *Naruto.*"

Star rolled her eyes. "Literally nobody asked you about whatever the hell you're talking about."

"Konoha is also known as the Hidden Leaf Village. It's revered for its lush, forested environment and is home to Naruto Uzumaki, the main character from the popular anime and manga series *Naruto.*"

"I said nobody asked! And don't act like you know anything about plants. The last time you were in my garden, you tried to smoke the basil!"

Dexter retorted with a grin, "In my defense, it got me pretty high."

Zane chuckled.

Dexter got serious. "But, for real though… You really think this is a good idea, Star? Demons seem to be trending wherever we take that book. You *really* want that in your house?"

"I don't think it matters anymore where we take the book. We're all going to die if we don't find that spell, and we're running out of options."

The house was packed with antiques. Curio cabinets displayed trinkets, and shelves were filled with books. Patterned wallpaper and gold-framed oil paintings lined the walls, their subjects looking on with judgment.

Star led them up the carpeted stairs to the third and final floor. They walked down a narrow hallway, the floorboards groaning under their weight. A cloying scent of rose perfume lingered in the air.

Zane noticed a door that was slightly open. Beyond it, a figure sat hunched in a rocking chair with her back to the doorway. Her brittle red hair was pulled into a bun. It had to be Star's grandmother. The creak of her chair synchronized with the ticking of a grandfather clock.

"Is that…?" Zane began, his voice low.

"Yeah, that's Grammy. Let me go talk to her," Star replied.

Dexter, eyeing her bloody clothes, asked, "Uh, maybe clean up first? Unless you're aiming to give her a heart attack."

Star waved him off. "She's practically blind with cataracts. She won't even notice."

She stepped into the room as the others waited in the doorway. Star knelt in front of her grandmother and spoke in a soft, gentle tone. The words were too low for the boys to hear, but suddenly, Grammy burst into hysterical laughter—raspy and unsettling. Her body shook violently in the chair.

Star wrapped a blanket around her grandmother's shoulders and pulled her into a hug, whispering something that finally calmed the woman down. Grammy's laughter faded into quiet murmurs as Star stood up and returned to the hallway.

"I don't think we're gonna get much out of her tonight," Star said. Grammy was still muttering something.

"Is she okay?" Zane asked.

"Yeah, just one of her episodes," Star said as she continued down the hallway. "This way, guys."

They followed, but the image of the cackling old woman in the rocking chair lingered in Zane's head.

Star welcomed them into her bedroom. "Wait here. I'm going to wash off this horror show." She grabbed some clothes from her dresser and then disappeared down the hallway.

Star's room added a youthful energy to the otherwise old house. Band posters from the '80s and '90s—like The Cure, Siouxsie and the Banshees, and Hole—covered the walls. Clothes were scattered across the floor, and a collection of Polaroid selfies decorated the cluttered desk. A stack of well-worn books, their pages dog-eared and covers faded, teetered on the bedside table.

A crystal vase on a bureau held a bouquet of roses, their petals brown and dry, but still pretty. Pink fairy lights around a vintage mirror added a dreamy touch.

In the corner, a little blue bird chirped melodiously in its cage.

"That's Merlin," Dexter explained. "He can actually talk a little."

"Oh, cool." Zane got closer and put his finger through the bars of the cage. The bird had a storybook appearance like he was from a Disney movie. "Hey, li'l dude, what's on your mind?"

"Watch out. He's a biter," Dexter warned.

"YUMMY, YUMMY!" the bird screeched before snapping at Zane's finger. Zane pulled back just in time, avoiding a nip as the bird collided with the cage.

"Whoa, noted."

"Told you," Dexter laughed as he sat on the edge of the bed. "Man, everything's so bonkers right now. I mean, what happened to Jake... I can't believe it. And you, with those crazy powers. You saved me again—you're my hero, twice over."

"I'm gettin' the hang of it, I think." Zane smiled. "Hunter... He kinda opened my eyes at the carnival. Showed me how to channel things, you know? Like, actually control what I've got going on instead of just freaking out." He looked up. "And after what happened to Jake... I'm all amped up."

He stretched his hands out. Tiny sparks crackled between his fingers.

"Dude, that's nuts. Straight outta Hogwarts!" Dexter leaned in, amazed. "Speaking of *sparks*... This Hunter guy, so you've gotten pretty tight?"

"Yeah," Zane admitted. "It's like, the moment I saw him, everything just... clicked. We have this insane connection. I mean, here's this random guy showing up in my dreams, talking about how he was literally made to find me, and then these powers—it's all so unreal. But when he explained it all to me tonight, it just made sense. Felt it right here," he said while tapping his chest.

"So, 'insane connection,' huh? Should I start calling you *Zunter* or *Hane?*"

Blush crept up Zane's cheeks. "Haha man, I don't know. Everything's so mixed up right now."

"It's funny, 'cause I always figured you and Star..." Before Dexter could finish his thought, Star was back.

She stood in the doorway, dressed in purple sweats, with a fluffy pink towel wrapped around her head like a cotton crown. Zane was caught off guard seeing her without makeup. She looked so innocent. He felt a pang in his heart for what could have been.

"Alright boys, let's get to it," Star declared, plopping down on the floor. "Anyone know Zoghrul?"

Zane and Dexter joined Star on the carpet, and they began their search through the journal.

"Hold up, I saw something before..." Zane flipped through the pages, stopping at the illustration of the emerald eye. "Look at this. That's what I saw on Hunter's chest."

Star studied the drawing. Beneath the picture was a small symbol of a key with a short line of text. She pointed at the scribbles with her acrylic fingernail. "This text here... What if it's an incantation or something? If this picture is connected to Hunter, these words could be the key to unlocking the spell. Zane, maybe you should try out your voice powers and read it out loud."

"I dunno. Hunter warned me not to mess around with Zoghrul. You saw what went down at the playground. You said it yourself—to stop with the chanting after I almost took you out with that bunny."

"I mean, Hunter told you the spell is hidden in this book, and that you have to unlock it. And there's literally a picture of a key right here. Do you have any other ideas?"

Zane sighed, "You're right. But, what if…"

"Get it together, Zane. The eclipse is less than 24 hours away. Just say it!"

Hunter told him that he had to do this on his own. He had to trust himself. Taking a slow breath, he recited the unfamiliar words, "*Unzar zeh pradzog.*"

The journal sprang to life, pages flipping on their own. The three friends watched as it stopped on a blank page. Words materialized, scrawled by an invisible hand. It was instructions for a potion. And below it, in Zoghrul, was what appeared to be the banishing spell.

Star clapped her hands together. "This is it! This is what we've been looking for!"

Dexter read the newly written text. "It's called, 'Elixir of Binding Chains.' It seems too good to be true."

"It does," Zane agreed. "Let's hope it works."

They studied the ingredients and steps for making the potion:

—

ELIXIR OF BINDING CHAINS

Gather ye these sacred components:

Venom of Serpent
With caution and reverence, procure the venom,
potent and perilous. Let it reside within a darkened
glass receptacle, shielded from the sight of the sun.

DEMON SUMMER

Berries of Deadly Nightshade
Under the dawn's early light, pluck the tender berries
of the deadly nightshade. Let them be harvested while
dew still adorns their baleful skin.

A Touch of Peppermint
Seek out the verdant leaves of fresh peppermint, or its
desiccated form, of the finest quality. The merest
whisper of its essence shall suffice.

The Precious Blood of a Descendant
With a sacrifice of self, draw forth three drops of the
blood of a descendant, ensuring the lineage is true and
untainted.

—

Follow these hallowed steps to conjure the elixir:

I.
In a cauldron, heat water drawn from a pristine
spring until it achieves a steady simmer. Intersperse
the liquid with three droplets of a descendant's blood,
intertwining their essences.

II.
In measured pace, pour the serpent's venom into the
heated liquid, and witness its transformation into a
deep, lustrous hue. With a wand carved of wood, stir
the brew in a clockwise circle, melding the venom with
its brethren.

III.

Cast the deadly nightshade berries into the churning potion, one by one. Behold the dazzling luminescence that emerges as the berries sink into the swirling depths.

IV.

Confer upon the potion the kiss of peppermint, by releasing its oils into the brew. Continue the clockwise stirring to harmonize the peppermint with the potion.

V.

Allow the concoction to cool, then strain it through a fine mesh or cloth, removing any remnants of corporeal matter. Preserve the completed potion within a vial of glass, sealed with a stopper.

The crafted elixir bestows its bearer the power to amplify or banish immense evil. Use it judiciously, for its potency endures but a fleeting span.

—

"Oh my God, we're like *so* lucky this recipe isn't in Zoghrul!" Star was excited. "As luck would have it, my grandmother totally grows deadly nightshade in our garden. She told me people call it 'belladonna.' Women used to put drops of the berry juice into their eyes to make them look wider and more seductive."

Dexter smirked, "Okay, Miss Britannica, you're on my team for the next botany trivia night."

"What about the other ingredients?" Zane pressed.

"Wait a second!" Dexter exclaimed, suddenly realizing something. "Madame Viola had all kinds of potions at her place. I'm pretty sure one of the bottles was labeled 'viper venom.' I thought it was super weird at the time, but now it totally makes sense—she probably had it for this exact reason."

Zane's face lit up. "Whoa, what're the chances? Hopefully, it's still there. That would cover two of the three ingredients. But what about the peppermint? Does your grandmother have that too, Star?"

"Ugh, no. It's basically like a weed and takes over the whole garden." Star thought for a moment. "Oh! What about peppermint tea? I bet they have some at Midnight Munchies. You know, the convenience store by Snaxtime. That should totally work, right?"

"Bonus points if we can find Celestial Seasonings brand," Dexter joked. "You know, *celestial*, for the lunar eclipse ritual… Get it?"

"We get it, Dex," Star groaned.

Before they could discuss anything further, their phones chimed in unison. A WhatsApp message from Marjorie appeared on their screens: *Team, there's been an incident at Snaxtime. We'll be closed while police investigate. Stay home and stay safe. I'll get back to you when I know more.*

The three friends knew all too well what had happened at Snaxtime.

"Alright, let's focus," Zane directed. "We split up; we each get one of the ingredients. I'll get the peppermint tea."

"I've got the berries covered," Star exclaimed.

Dexter grimaced, realizing he would have to retrieve the snake venom from the psychic's parlor, another heinous crime scene. "Guess it's back to the house of horrors for me. You two are too kind."

With the tomb below Snaxtime and the kitchen having the tools they needed for the potion, they decided to meet back there before midnight. They would then do the banishing ritual during the full-blood lunar eclipse.

Zane and Dexter rose from the floor. "Alright, let's do it," Dexter said. He looked at Star. "I guess you're not driving me, huh?"

"Sorry, Dex. Your private car service isn't open this early. I think there's a bike against the shed out front."

Dexter gave her a look. "Thanks, Star. I've been meaning to start my training for the Tour de France."

Zane waved his skateboard. "I've got my own wheels."

They exited into the hallway, leaving Star in her bedroom. Zane noticed that Grammy's door was now closed.

They went down the stairs and out the front door. The sun was rising.

"You good?" Zane asked Dexter, grabbing his skateboard from under his arm.

"For sure, I got this. See you at Snaxtime." Dexter gave a two-finger salute as Zane kick-pushed off and sped down the hill.

Now on his own, Dexter searched for the bike. He found it by the shed. "Perfect," he muttered. But then he saw the flat tires and missing seat. "Just perfect," he sighed.

Heading to the back of the house, he saw something both funny and sad—a tiny pink kids' bike with training wheels and tattered streamers on the handles.

Dexter tightened the straps of his backpack, pushed up his glasses, and smoothed back his curls. Despite the bike's condition, he mounted it and got on his way, fully aware of the absurdity of the situation.

He shook his head to himself. At the beginning of the summer, he was an inconsequential fry cook. But now, here he was, pedaling on the horizon of the apocalypse with the fate of the world resting on his shoulders.

CHAPTER ELEVEN

he first thing Dexter noticed when he arrived at Madame Viola's house was how much it had changed. It seemed to have aged years overnight. The paint was peeling off, exposing decayed wood. The garden was overrun with weeds.

Dexter stopped in front of the locked iron gate that guarded the entrance. The metal was rusted. He started climbing, his sneakers struggling for a grip on the decrepit bars. As he lifted himself over, his jeans snagged and tore on a jagged edge. He felt the bite of metal on his skin. He hadn't just ripped his pants, he'd also cut himself. He pushed aside the pain and landed on the other side. Blood was running down his leg.

He took a moment to survey the yard. The garden was a wasteland. A lone, bare tree stood in the center.

Yellow tape crisscrossed the premises, and evidence markers dotted the ground. Between whatever happened after they left and the police combing the scene for evidence, Dexter could only hope the ingredient was still there.

He climbed the stairs of the wraparound porch. The charms that once hung above the front door were now strewn about on the ground in broken fragments. The door was locked. He would need to find another way in.

Dexter circled to the side of the house and spotted a cracked-open window. Despite his efforts, it wouldn't budge.

He found a garden shovel in a pile of planting tools. He wedged it beneath the window and pried it open with a grunt.

Dexter squeezed through the narrow gap and pushed past the curtains. He clumsily entered, landing head-first on the floor and smashing the right side of his glasses. He picked himself up and took a moment to assess his surroundings. It was hard to see through his cracked lens.

Dexter had stood in this very spot before, but it felt entirely different now. A musty scent made him a little queasy.

The room was a disaster, showing signs of a violent struggle. Dexter crept toward the shelves where he had seen the bottle of viper venom. Many of the bottles had been knocked to the floor and shattered. He prayed that the snake venom was not among them.

As he drew closer to the shelf, a shadow flitted past him. Dexter froze in place. He wasn't alone. His eyes darted around the room.

The sound of breaking glass pierced the silence. He spun around to locate the source, but the disarray made it hard to identify. He needed to find the vial of venom and get out of there, fast. Zane wasn't here to save him this time.

He turned back to the shelves, his heart pounding so loudly he thought it might give him away. He spotted the vial of snake venom and reached out with a shaking hand.

As he clutched it, a figure sprang from the darkness and landed at his feet. Startled, Dexter screamed and dropped the vial.

It was just Madame Viola's cat, staring at him with hungry eyes. "Whoa, you scared me, little buddy."

The vial! Dexter realized it might not have survived the fall. "Crap." Dexter got on his knees, searching the floor through his busted glasses.

Fortunately, he found it intact and shoved it in his backpack. Mission accomplished.

The cat brushed against him and meowed.

"Aw, it's all gonna be okay." But as he spoke, he doubted his own words. Did he believe them himself? Getting the potion ingredients was stressful but felt minor compared to the monumental challenge of banishing a demon. It seemed he was telling half-truths to both the cat and himself.

"Are you hungry?" he asked, picturing the cat alone in this abandoned house. Dexter rummaged through his backpack and found a Slim Jim. He unwrapped it, broke it into pieces, and put them on the ground. "Bet you'll like this." He gave the cat one last pet.

Dexter maneuvered his way to the front door. He unlocked it, ducked under the police tape, and stepped out into the blinding daylight. He took one last glance at the house before moving on, sending a final wish for its solitary inhabitant.

He looked down at his torn jeans, stained and still damp with blood. The wound throbbed, but he barely minded. Feeling pain reminded him that he was alive. He could've easily ended up like Jake. He still could.

Dexter got on the bike and began to pedal back home, where he'd try to get some much-needed rest before tonight's ritual.

Star sat at her vanity, sweeping a hairbrush through her red tresses. Her task was simpler compared to Zane's and Dexter's, yet her nerves buzzed like bees.

The Emberheart name held deep roots in the town's history. Star's parents, globe-trotting art collectors, were more frequently spotted in glossy magazines than in their own household. Star's grandmother took on the role of raising her. In her heyday, Grammy was a celebrated beauty whose charm had captivated many before she ultimately chose to settle down with Star's grandfather.

As the sole heir to this storied lineage, Star was often overshadowed by the expectations tied to her family's reputation. But recently, she had started finding her groove. That's one of the reasons she loved working at Snaxtime. There, she shed the weight of being Starling Rose Emberheart. She could just be Star, her sassy self. The extra spending cash was always fun, although she certainly didn't need it.

She'd actually had fun this summer. She almost felt guilty allowing Dexter and Zane to get so close to her. She had been so guarded her entire life, feeling like an imposter among common folk. Oh boy, that Zane was cute, though.

But she'd never lost focus. She knew more than anyone the importance of upholding her family's heritage. She loved Grammy more than anything, and she'd never let her down.

Her grandmother mostly stayed in her quarters on the top floor of the mansion, no longer well enough to spend much time outside. She still managed to bake now and then and occasionally wandered out to her beloved garden, though far less often than she used to.

This green oasis had been Star's classroom, where she learned to identify various herbs and blooms under her grandmother's tutelage. Star felt a shared bond in their love for botany.

She looked out her window at the beautiful garden below. The first light of dawn stretched across the groomed lawns and colorful flowerbeds. According to the journal, it was crucial to gather the berries during this early hour. She opened Merlin's cage and set him free. The little blue bird followed her outside.

Grammy's garden was a labyrinth of green trails that led to individual sections, each boasting an assortment of exotic flora. Trellises with flowering vines created natural archways. Nearby, fountains added to the garden's serenity, their shimmering waters scattering fragments of morning light onto the neighboring plants.

Star skipped through the garden, leaving wet footprints on the cobblestones from the morning dew. Merlin fluttered alongside her. She offered her hand, and he perched upon it. "Can you believe it, Merlin? It's all finally coming together. I can just taste it."

"Yummy, yummy," he chirped.

Star's steps carried her to the very back of the garden, to an old, high stone wall draped in a cloak of thick ivy. She moved aside the green curtain to reveal a door. She pulled an oversized key from her pocket and inserted it into the lock. The door creaked open, revealing a hidden sanctuary.

Within this secluded space, several crumbling headstones marked her ancestors' graves. At the entrance of a small mausoleum stood an imposing bronze statue of her great-grandfather. The statue seemed almost alive, as if his ghost was watching over the generations.

"Good morning, Papa." Here, Star felt a deep connection to her roots.

The night-blooming flowers grew beside the mausoleum. She hummed a lullaby Grammy used to sing as she plucked the deadly nightshade berries. Merlin circled above her, chirping along to her song.

Tonight was a test of faith and fate. Star would help banish the demon and save humanity, or she could be responsible for letting Demonika rule forever.

She sensed the winds of change gathering, and melancholy washed over her for the simpler times of her past. She remembered the curious girl who had absorbed her grandmother's wisdom among these very blooms. Here, she had always found peace when the world seemed too big. And now, standing on the brink of an uncertain future, Star cherished these memories more than ever.

But Star also knew it was time for her to grow. She was no longer that naive little girl.

Casting one last look across the garden, Star pivoted on her heel and navigated back to the house, cradling the basket of berries. She was one step closer to the crossroads of destiny, her resolve firmly rooted, just like the plants in Grammy's garden.

Breakfast awaited her—Grammy's signature orange blossom cake. She could already taste the moist, golden delight topped with creamy frosting and orange blossom sugar.

If she was lucky, a few precious hours of sleep would precede tonight's events, a pause in time she could really use.

As an orphan who'd jumped from one home to another, Zane had always fantasized about a connection to his past, some link that would make him feel less alone in this world. Now, with the knowledge of his true heritage, he was a bit freaked out.

Zane figured getting the peppermint tea leaves would be easy, so he decided to head home first and look into his family history.

He had only scratched the surface of his great uncle's stuff. The attic was packed full of boxes begging to be searched.

His new house was a charming, single-story structure. It was quaint and inviting, clad in fresh white paint. The front door was framed by two matching windows, like eyes, giving the house an almost face-like appearance.

Inside, the floors, walls, and ceiling were covered with wooden panels. It was clear that his great-uncle had preserved the rustic beauty with care. The bookshelves held an impressive collection of literature.

The attic was a vault of memories. Zane dug through a box of keepsakes and found a stack of old photo albums. One of them was filled with sepia-toned pictures of his parents when they were younger. He'd only ever had the one photo of them in his wallet, so seeing these new images felt like uncovering a hidden treasure.

His mother's bright smile, his dad's light eyes—just like his—jumped out at him. But what really grabbed his attention were the strange details: in so many of the pictures, they were wearing hooded robes, surrounded by others dressed the same.

Zane immersed himself deeper into the album's pages, discovering an extensive visual chronicle of his parents' lives. He found himself witness to ceremonial gatherings, celebrations, and intimate snapshots of joy. For the first time, Zane felt a connection to who they were.

His investigation led him to a newspaper clipping hidden between the pages. It described a tragic accident—a mysterious fiery explosion on the town's outskirts that killed his parents. He had never known the details of their deaths. The article was vague and provided no clear answers, only raising more questions. With the threat of Demonika looming, he decided to leave this puzzle unsolved for now, but silently vowed to return to it once their mission was completed.

He continued searching through the piles and came across a marble box. He wiped away a thick layer of dust with his shirt, revealing a jewel-encrusted surface. He opened the lid.

Nestled within the box was a gold ring. Its band boasted a large emerald cut in the shape of an eye, similar to the one on Hunter's chest and the illustration in the journal.

Zane slid the ring onto his finger. It fit perfectly.

Beneath the ring lay a surprise—an envelope bearing Zane's name. His heart hammered as he unfolded the letter.

Dearest Zane,

For a lifetime, I have remained a stranger to protect you. However, if you now hold this letter, it signifies my absence from this world and, thus, the cessation of my guardianship. I am Reginald, your great-uncle, and it is my duty to reveal to you the profound truth of our ancestry.

Our quaint town holds a past steeped in the mystical and the ancient. Long ago, it was plagued by an insidious demon named Demonika. The burden of standing against this demon, of safeguarding our town and its unsuspecting residents, has been carried forward by our family, the Hawthorns, through many generations. Each member has stood vigilant as a warrior against the malevolent force threatening our peaceful existence. These are the responsibilities we are bound to, our legacy and our duty.

The ring that now graces your finger is more than a mere trinket. It symbolizes our family's pledge and serves as both a shield against the corrosive power of the demon and an amplifier of your own strength when called upon. It has belonged to many of our ancestors. This ring, imbued with generations of our family's resolve, will not only protect you but also enhance your innate abilities in times of need. Hold it close, always. Remember, within you lies not only the strength and bravery necessary to confront any threat but also the potential to rise above it, magnified by the legacy carried in this ring.

I deeply regret that we never met in person. I hid you from this life to honor my promise to your parents to keep you safe. But now, you are the last heir tasked with protecting humankind. I have unwavering faith in your ability to continue our family's mission. Remember, you are not alone in this journey. Allies stand ready to join you in the battle against darkness.

Let the beacon of our forebears guide you through this journey.

With love and hope,
Your Great-Uncle Reginald

Zane read and reread Reginald's words, confirming his new mission—a destiny beyond anything he could have imagined.

Tears formed in Zane's eyes as the weight of sleeplessness and the significance of his circumstances overwhelmed him. The ring felt heavy on his finger. It all became too intense. He took it off and tucked it into his pocket.

Zane's phone buzzed. He had set his alarm earlier. He realized, with a jolt, that the whole day had slipped by since he started his attic exploration. It was already dark outside. He still needed to get the peppermint tea leaves, and the eclipse was fast approaching.

Zane weaved past the scattered boxes, went downstairs, and stepped outside. With his skateboard underfoot, he hurried toward the convenience store. He thought about his parents.

I'll make you both proud of me.

⸻ C ⸻

CHAPTER TWELVE

Midnight Munchies was the ultimate snack destination. Its purple and orange neon lights usually drew in late-night stoners. But under tonight's full moon, it was empty.

Inside, a slushy machine purred in the corner, its frosty chambers churning with candy-colored swirls. Hot dogs spun on the grill, while fresh donuts sat in a case waiting to be eaten. They smelled delicious together. Overhead, fluorescent bulbs buzzed, and K-pop music piped in from ceiling speakers.

Zane wandered the aisles. His heavy eyes swept over the snacks that vied for his attention. Rows of chocolate bars, bags of chips, and pastel-colored candies winked at him. He walked past chocolate-covered pretzels, neon gummies, jumbo marshmallows, and cookies filled with creme. The place was a Disneyland of junk food, where diets went to die.

All of the colorful packaging tempted him to forget his mission. On any regular night, Zane would've been down for a candy binge. But he had bigger fish to fry.

He headed to the hot beverage station. Next to the coffee and hot water carafes, he found a selection of tea packets. There was chamomile, Earl Grey, green tea, chai, and even jasmine, but no peppermint. There was a noticeable gap where it should have been.

He approached the front counter to ask for help. The woman behind the register had brassy hair and chipped pink nails. Her chubby fingers tapped rhythmically against the countertop, and her eyes were half-open as if struggling to stay awake.

"Excuse me," Zane said, trying to mask his urgency. "You got any peppermint tea?"

The worker stared into space. Zane tried again, "Hello??"

She replied with a series of nondescript grunts and a juicy burp. The stench was pungent, like sour milk and rotten eggs. Zane took a step back and covered his nose.

"I really need peppermint tea. It looks like you're out over there." He pointed to the coffee station.

The store's lights fluttered on and off, and the music became erratic, slowing down and speeding up.

The woman's eyes popped wide, and she straightened

up like a jack-in-the-box.

"Ummm, ma'am?"

A bulge ascended her chest into her throat. Her skin creaked like strained rubber as her jaw extended freakishly wide.

A small green head with pink eyes emerged from her mouth. It made squishing sounds as it rose.

Zane recognized the creature. It belonged to the demon's vile horde. It bared its jagged, mangled teeth as it erupted into a wild, hyena-like laugh.

The woman's body slumped beneath it, falling to the floor like a puppet with cut strings, dead. The ghoul, now proudly stationed on top of the counter, shifted its insane hysterics into a throaty growl. Zane stumbled backward and fell into a snack pie display.

The abomination launched itself at Zane, who threw his hands out to orchestrate a counterattack. The store came to life as he telepathically shot cans, bottles, and boxes through the air, pelting the creature from all directions. For a moment, it seemed like the barrage might overpower the monster.

But the ghoul twisted its wiry body, dodging the convenience storm. It bore down on him, teeth ready.

Zane grabbed his skateboard and swung it like a bat. The beast recoiled from the impact, giving Zane just the window he needed. He jumped to his feet and bolted toward the exit.

With escape in sight, Zane's eyes locked onto a pack of peppermint gum beneath the counter. It was a far cry from the tea leaves he'd intended to find, but in desperate times, he'd have to improvise. He swiped the gum and sprinted outside.

The goblin blasted through the glass storefront in a hailstorm of glittering shards. It rolled, landed, and then prowled toward him on all fours. Its monstrous grunts grew louder with every stride, closing in with alarming speed.

Zane couldn't outrun it. Midstride, he reached into his pocket and slammed the emerald ring onto his finger. He skidded to a halt, turned, and thrust his hands toward the shrieking ghoul.

The jewel ignited, unleashing a violent flash of green light that enveloped the creature and froze it in place. It squealed, spasmed, and with a gruesome pop, it exploded into a cloud of viscous bile and goo, showering the parking lot in smoking entrails.

"Whoa." Zane looked down at his ring. "Serious power-up! Thanks, Uncle Reg."

He vaulted onto his skateboard and propelled himself away from Midnight Munchies. Hopefully the gum would be potent enough to do the trick.

After his successful mission and some much-needed sleep, Dexter was the first of the three friends to return to

Snaxtime. He made his grand entrance astride the children's bicycle. The prized bottle of snake venom was in his backpack, nestled between a comic book and a bag of Fritos.

Dexter parked the bike and hung his backpack on the handlebars. He pulled out his phone and sent a message to Zane and Star: *ETA?*

But it didn't go through. He had no service. That was unusual. Snaxtime always had reliable coverage.

From overhead, a sudden and terrifying shriek ripped through the air.

Dexter looked up. A small green ghoul sat perched on a tree branch. It had bat-like wings and a single eyeball in the center of its face. It emitted another shriek and shot down at him.

The world turned into a nightmarish kaleidoscope through Dexter's cracked glasses. The monster multiplied into an army of swooping terrors in his skewed vision.

Dexter ran for his life.

The flying goblin's sharp talons latched onto his fluffy hair like a bird of prey. Dexter swatted at the cyclops and broke free. His foot skidded on the loose gravel, nearly sending him crashing to the ground. Luckily, he regained his footing and bolted toward the wooded area behind Snaxtime.

In that moment, he remembered the bully, Mike Henderson. He was tired of running. Enough was enough. Dexter balled his fists and spun around to meet the goblin head-on, ready to fight. "COME ON!"

Just as the words slipped from his mouth, the monster struck him like a bullet.

When Zane got to the restaurant, it was almost eleven. Even though it was late, the full moon lit up everything like it was daytime. Police tape flapped in the breeze.

Something grabbed him from behind and squeezed him tight.

"There you are." It was Star.

"Where's Dexter?" Zane asked.

"He's not here yet. And my phone's not working."

Zane noticed something. "Is that…"

"Dexter's backpack!" Star exclaimed. They ran over to it. His bag lay open on the ground next to the child's bike. "That's my bike from when I was little. Weird… I told him to use the other one. I didn't mean this!" If Dexter had been there, she would've teased him about it.

She rummaged through the backpack. "Oh my God." She pulled out the vial of venom and held it up. "He got it! But why would he just leave it here?"

"This isn't right." Zane spun around. "Dexter!" He looked at his phone. "I don't have any bars either."

She shook her head. "It's like we're in a total dead zone."

"We gotta find him," Zane insisted.

Star's attention snapped up to the looming eclipse. "Look! It's happening. We don't have time to look for Dex."

"We can't do this without him."

Star clenched the vial. "We're *all* done for if we don't make this potion right now."

She was right. They had to rescue their town from the clutches of darkness, even if it meant pressing on without one of their own.

They hurried into Snaxtime. Fortunately, the power was back on, but the place was still a complete mess from the night before. They ransacked the kitchen for the tools needed for the potion. Each item they found was a triumph: a soup pot to be used as a cauldron, a wooden spoon to function as a wand, a dish rag for straining the potion, and an empty glass ketchup bottle to serve as a vial.

Star set the snake venom on the counter. She rifled through her purse and pulled out a mason jar with the deadly nightshade berries. "Alright, hand over the tea."

"So, something crazy happened."

Star gave him a look.

"I was attacked. At Midnight Munchies… It was one of Demonika's minions."

Star's hands lost grip on the jar, which clattered onto the counter as she moved closer to Zane. "Oh my God, are you okay?"

"It was like a horror movie. It just burst right out of the cashier. It, like, literally exploded out of her mouth."

"Her *mouth!?*" Star's face drained of color.

"Yeah. It was..."

"But you *did* get the tea, right?" Star interrupted.

Zane sighed, pulling the pack of gum from his pocket. "No tea, but I got this. It's peppermint gum."

Star snatched it out of his hand. "*Gum*, Zane? The recipe called for 'the finest quality' peppermint. We're going to save the world with *Wrigley's?*"

Zane shrugged in defeat. "It says 'naturally flavored' on the label."

"This can't be happening," she huffed in annoyance.

"It's all we got."

She sighed. "Okay, let's just hope this gum's got enough peppermint kick to do the trick."

They followed the instructions in the journal:

> *In a cauldron, heat water drawn from a pristine*
> *spring until it achieves a steady simmer.*

They placed the soup pot on the stove. Star emptied several bottles of spring water into the pot before turning up the heat.

> *Intersperse the liquid with three droplets of a*
> *descendant's blood, intertwining their essences.*

"So, Mr. Descendant, ready to donate some of that top-shelf blood of yours?" Star asked.

"Do I get a cookie after?" Zane reached for his keychain and unfolded a pocketknife. He pricked the tip of his pointer finger. A bead of blood formed, and with a mere wince, he let three droplets fall into the now-boiling water.

In measured pace, pour the serpent's venom into the heated liquid, and witness its transformation into a deep, lustrous hue. With a wand carved of wood, stir the brew in a clockwise circle, melding the venom with its brethren.

They poured the serpent's venom into the pot. It sank into the liquid before turning it an opaque black. Zane stirred the brew clockwise as the journal dictated. The mixture became glossy and thick.

Cast the deadly nightshade berries into the churning potion, one by one. Behold the dazzling luminescence that emerges as the berries sink into the swirling depths.

Star handed Zane the open jar. One at a time, he plopped the berries into the pot, and the concoction turned a glowing purple.

Confer upon the potion the kiss of peppermint, by releasing its oils into the brew. Continue the clockwise stirring to harmonize the peppermint with the potion.

Zane unwrapped a few sticks of gum and chewed them, trying to extract as much flavor as he could without swallowing. After milking the gum for all it was worth, he spat into the bubbling brew. He kept stirring, praying with each rotation that the gum would work.

Allow the concoction to cool, then strain it through a fine mesh or cloth, removing any remnants of corporeal matter. Preserve the completed potion within a vial of glass, sealed with a stopper.

They both blew on it to cool it down, then strained it through the dish rag, funneled it into the empty ketchup bottle, and screwed on the cap to seal their creation.

Zane held up the bottle to inspect it. It wasn't perfect, not by a long shot. But it was the best they could muster under the circumstances.

"So," Zane began. "What do we do now?"

"We need to go down to the basement and get ready for the ritual," Star directed. "The tomb is under the restaurant—the closer we are to it, the better."

"Okay, let's go." Zane led the way downstairs with Star right behind him.

Out of nowhere, a powerful blow to the back of Zane's head blindsided him.

In an instant, everything went black.

———— O ————

CHAPTER THIRTEEN

Zane's eyes fluttered open. His head was throbbing. He tried to focus on his surroundings. *Where am I?*

Towering columns rose from the floor to a vaulted ceiling covered in a mosaic of golden tiles. The room was lit by torches, their flames green. The walls were etched with glowing runes and glyphs.

Murals spanned the walls, depicting a harrowing tale. Villagers, their faces twisted in fear, battled a powerful demon. The sequence of images showed the demon's journey from dominance to defeat and capture. The last painting depicted the demon imprisoned, her eyes ablaze with rage.

He was in Demonika's tomb.

Zane tried to move. "Ahhh!" He was immobilized, his wrists bound by iron cuffs and chains secured to the wall above his head. His shirt was gone, and his chest was exposed to the cold air. His jeans were in tatters. Panic washed over him as the grim reality of his predicament became clear.

He scanned the tomb. *Dexter.* His friend was stripped and chained against a distant wall.

Zane tried to construct a coherent sequence of events that could have led to this moment. How had they ended up here? Desperation swept through him. Gathering the remnants of his strength, he shouted, "DEXTER!"

Dexter didn't respond. The weak rise and fall of his chest was the only sign he was still alive.

Zane's muscles tensed as he tried to break free from his restraints. But the chains were unyielding. The cuffs bit into his flesh with each unsuccessful tug. There was no way out.

"Hi, Zane," a voice called out from the shadows.

Star?

She entered, barefoot and moving like a panther. A purple silk robe hugged her voluptuous form, and her hair flowed over her shoulders in a cascade of molten lava.

"Always finding yourself in the darkest places. You're so emo," Star purred while flitting her fingers in the air. She ambled toward him with a provocative sway. "A bit tied up, are we? Honestly, not your best look."

With the points of her blood-red fingernails, she traced a path down his bare torso. Zane gasped, and his muscles recoiled.

She was wearing his ring.

"What's the matter, Z? Cat got your tongue?" Star teased.

"Star… what's going on?"

She dramatically pulled her hand away and placed it over her heart. "Oh, didn't anyone tell you? Whoops, my bad. Let me explain. It turns out I *am* kinda like a princess, after all. My great-grandfather was the King of fast food himself, Harold Snaxton. Grammy's daddy. So, yeah, I'm a Snaxton too—a bona fide Burger Queen."

Zane wriggled in his chains. "What the…"

"You know our demon problem? She's actually the one who's gonna save us all. My family's been serving her for like a thousand years. And tonight, we're finally bringing her back to power. Crazy, right?"

Zane's mind spun, trying to keep pace with the avalanche of revelation. "Wait, you're telling me you're in that cult? And you worship that… that *DEMON!?*"

"We're not your run-of-the-mill demon worshippers, Zane. And we're not just some basic cult, either. We're a *family*, devoted to raising our Queen, Demonika, back to life, once and for all, *forever* this time. To give her back what's rightfully hers: dominion over human-ville.

"And honestly, can you blame us? *Men* have had their shot and, like, totally screwed it up. The planet's dying, everyone's miserable. It's time for a change. A fresh start with a woman in charge. Girl Power, baby. And surprise, surprise, you've been part of the plan all along."

"Me?" The word barely made it out of Zane's throat. "What the *hell* are you talking about?"

"Oh, it's all about Hell." She brushed her fingers through his hair. "Hell's coming up to party, and it's gonna be epic. And you, Zane, you're not just some rando skater boy. You're the real deal, the chosen one. The Hawthorn family's magic is legendary. It's been chilling in your DNA your whole life, waiting for this very moment. We needed your power to cut her chains. You're, like, basically our savior."

She moved in closer, her voice dropping to a near-whisper. "And now that we have that power, there's absolutely nothing standing in our way." Star pecked him on the cheek.

"I almost forgot to thank you for my new statement piece." She flaunted the emerald ring. "I just love how it brings out the color in my eyes."

With his hands bound and without his ring, Zane was powerless.

Star gestured toward a rune etched on the wall. It pulsed with a green light. "See that? I used your precious ring to set up a little barrier. No outside powers can penetrate this tomb. So don't expect your pathetic boyfriend to crash our little shindig."

Hunter.

"Plot twist," she said, revealing the ketchup bottle from her robe. "We were never gonna use this potion to banish her. This is for our dark queen's big comeback tour. But first, we're going to have a little dinner party. And you're tonight's special, the catch of the day!" She winked. "Word on the street is that you're *magically delicious*."

Zane hung against the stone wall, numb.

"I'll be honest, I might've been crushing on you, just a little bit." Her lips curled downward. "But, like, when destiny calls, you can't just hit ignore, right?"

A distant grunt caught Star's attention, pulling her gaze into the darkness. She turned back to Zane with a devilish look in her eye. "How exciting! We have a *very* special guest with us tonight."

Zane strained his eyes, trying to make out what was lurking in the shadows. Star vanished into the distance and reemerged with a wheelchair. Slouched in it was a figure more corpse than living being. Although Zane had previously only seen her from behind, he recognized Grammy. Her eyes were cloudy and white, and her mouth hung open. Drool pooled at its corners. Star's blue bird, Merlin, was perched on her shoulder.

Grammy was in a shiny gold dress with ruffled sleeves. She had a pearl necklace and clip-on earrings that made her earlobes sag nearly to her shoulders. Smeared red lipstick gave her lips the illusion of fullness.

Star tapped Grammy's cheek. "Grammy insisted on wearing her favorite party dress. Doesn't she look pretty? She's basically been waiting her entire life for this day. And trust me, that's been, like, a really, *really* long time."

In a grotesque gesture, Grammy's tongue darted out to lick her hungry lips.

"Oh, Grammy, don't worry! We'll save you a bite." Star cupped her hand to her mouth as if telling Zane a secret. "She doesn't look it, but she can really pack it away." She patted her grandmother's emaciated belly. "I mean, really, girl, where do you put it all?"

"YUMMY, YUMMY!" Merlin squawked.

"Yes, Merlin, you'll get the leftovers."

Zane thrashed in his chains.

Star closed her eyes and reset her posture. She took a deep, meditative breath and exhaled. "Now, let's get this party started."

She began to chant and dance. Her slow movements accentuated her sensual curves. The front slit of her robe parted, offering glimpses of her long, smooth legs.

The ring glowed on her finger.

Star's chant grew more chaotic. She whipped her hair from side to side while her arms undulated like twin serpents through the air. Ribbons of electricity circled around her as she cast her spell.

Scores of the now-familiar ghouls surfaced. They joined her in song, their discordant voices merging into a powerful chorus.

As the concert unfolded, a coil of green mist coalesced around Star. Behind her, bolts of red lightning flashed.

The mist grew denser, turning into a turbulent vortex. Then, from the eye of the storm, Demonika appeared.

Her hair whirled around her like snakes. Her lips split apart in a croaky cackle, revealing razor-sharp teeth. Gray skin stretched taut over her gaunt face.

Star sank to her knees, bending in worship. "My Queen, I've brought you the ultimate sacrifice—the *descendant*. We're ready for your final ascension."

Blue flames shot from the demon's eyes.

"Oh, and there's an appetizer, too," Star said as the demon turned to Dexter.

Zane cried out, "DEXTER! DEXTER!"

Dexter stirred.

"I figured you'd be extra hungry." Star was proud of herself.

Demonika's forked tongue slithered across her lips. "Mmmm."

Zane shouted in desperation, "Star, stop this! He's our friend—he *loves* you!"

Star turned back to Zane with a mock pout. "Awww, Zane, that's so adorable," she cooed. "Still clinging to the idea of friendship? I love that for you. Too bad friendship isn't on the menu tonight. You two, however? Totally are." Star waved goodbye to Dexter. "Later, tater tot."

Demonika's jaw stretched wide enough to devour Dexter whole.

"DEXTER!!!"

Then, in a heartbeat, her mouth snapped shut around him with a clash.

And just like that, Dexter's final story played out on the main stage of the end of the world.

"NOOOOOO!" Zane's vision blurred with tears.

The crunching of bones drowned out Zane's sobs as the monster polished off her hors d'oeuvre.

Demonika bellowed as Dexter's soul fed her power. She threw her arms back and flew higher into the air. Dark, leathery wings unfurled from her spine as she doubled in size. Her black hair turned blue, and her gray skin morphed into the same ghastly green of her ghouls. Her cackles turned into a roar.

She raised her hands. Her fingers snapped, crackled, and popped, elongating into talons.

She turned her attention to Zane, and with a slow, drawn-out growl, she said, "And now for the main course!"

Demonika flew toward Zane. His muscles clenched in anticipation.

She licked his sweaty bicep. Her tongue felt like sandpaper. "Tough and strong," she hissed. "But I prefer my meat tender."

Demonika then commanded in Zoghrul, "*ZAR KHUL NAZHT TORMAI!*"

Her talons lit up like tasers as she plunged them into Zane's ribs, sending electric shocks through his body. The current surged up the chains that bound his wrists. The metal sparked and seared his flesh as he convulsed violently against the wall.

The demon twisted her claws inside him before ripping them out. She brought her nails to her lips and savored the blood with her serpentine tongue. "Delicious."

The tomb's ceiling erupted open to reveal the full-blood lunar eclipse occurring above them. The critters climbed up the sides of the tomb in droves. Their writhing forms melded together, transforming the walls into a squirming membrane.

Star cradled the potion to her bosom. Her high-pitched laughter was on the brink of hysteria.

Zane was hopeless. There was no escape.

The ring!

The ring could amplify his power. He had to get it back.

Zane recalled Hunter's lesson on voice command. Though he had struggled with it at the carnival, it was his only hope.

"Return to me!"

The ring remained on Star's finger.

She laughed mockingly. "Oh no, Zane, did your little magic trick go poof?"

Grieving for Dexter, Zane's desperation fueled his resolve. The words surged out of him instinctively in Zoghrul, *"XATHAR VORUUN!"* His voice vibrated with power.

The crescent-shaped birthmark on his chest—the one Star had noticed earlier that summer at the lake—blazed to life, glowing with an ancient energy. The ring quivered on Star's hand before rocketing off and locking onto his finger.

It worked. Perfectly. He finally had command over Zoghrul.

Hunter, I need you.

The ring ignited, and everything froze. Reality warped and twisted. Zane found himself floating amongst crystalline clouds.

He'd been here once before.

Hunter materialized. His stone-white skin glittered. The emerald eye on his chest throbbed and glistened as he spoke, "The full-blood moon eclipse is upon us. We must combine our powers."

Hunter thrust himself into Zane. The feeling was euphoric.

Almost as swiftly as he had left, Zane was transported back to Demonika's crypt. The monster was once again advancing toward him.

But Zane felt different. He looked down at himself, noting the impressive stature his form had taken. His physique was now rippling with rock-hard muscle. His skin was flawless and smooth.

Hunter's eye-shaped emerald now sat embedded in Zane's chest. A jolt of power surged within him. His muscles swelled—a display of might that pulverized the shackles confining him. He landed on the ground and pivoted to face Demonika.

She laughed, her dark wings undulating in the air. "Futile, human," she snarled. "Your new form will only make me stronger when I consume you."

Demonika threw out her hands. "*ZAR KUL THRAKA ORMOS!*" She conjured a glowing orb and hurled it at Zane. It struck him with brutal impact, sending him flying back. He crashed onto the ground near Star.

Star jumped back and dropped the potion on the floor.

She darted toward the fallen bottle, but Zane was faster. He extended his arm and opened his hand. Like a magnet, it flew into his grip.

Demonika lunged at him.

Zane hurled the bottle into the demon's path. It shattered onto the ground, releasing a shaft of intense light. She froze mid-air, her face scrunching in pain as she struggled against the invisible force restraining her.

The eclipse was now perfectly aligned in the sky.

Zane levitated and locked eyes with the demon, who was held captive in the prison of light.

He traced intricate symbols in the air with his hands, the motions coming to him without thought. The banishing incantation from the journal poured from his lips. It was as if the words had been etched into his memory:

"SHADU LIPRA, THIG RESH!"

A shockwave of green energy blasted from Zane's chest. It struck Demonika with the power of a detonating star, and she let out a feral cry. Her wail carried the torment of a thousand trapped souls.

Acid spewed from her mouth, splashing onto Grammy and Merlin.

The bird disintegrated instantly. Grammy's skin bubbled and melted as she convulsed in her wheelchair. Within seconds, a smoldering, skeletal husk was all that remained.

"GRAMMY!!!" Star screamed in agony.

A bejeweled sarcophagus burst from the ground and opened. Green smoke swirled around Demonika and her horde of grotesqueries, pulling them toward the coffin like a genie drawn back into its bottle. The lid slammed shut, sealing them inside.

A magical inscription carved itself into the marble surface. The sarcophagus lowered back into the ground.

An aftershock rumbled through the tomb, tossing Star like a rag doll.

Zane fell to the floor and landed on his back. As the dust settled, he saw Star's lifeless form in the distance.

In a jolt, his arms flung wide, and his back arched as Hunter exited his body. The pain was excruciating like being torn from within. But then it released.

Hunter slumped beside him, weak but conscious. The emerald was back on his chest.

The crypt trembled beneath them.

"The tomb is sealing shut. We must hurry before you are trapped," Hunter instructed as he struggled to sit up.

"Okay, let's get out of here!" Zane got up and tugged Hunter by the hand. But Hunter didn't move.

"I must stay. This is my duty—to watch over Demonika," Hunter said.

Zane understood, but it crushed him. Gratitude and devastation warred in his chest as he looked into Hunter's eyes. He knelt and embraced him tightly. "It's been epic."

"*Totally* epic," Hunter replied, pulling him close. "You have fulfilled your destiny. Remember me."

Zane placed his hand over Hunter's heart. "Forever."

Hunter waved his arm through the air. A stone stairwell appeared, leading up from the crypt and offering Zane a path to safety.

"Go now," Hunter commanded.

With visible effort, Hunter rose to his feet. He squared his shoulders, standing tall. His green eyes turned gray as his body stiffened into marble.

Zane approached the statue. He caressed Hunter's stone cheek. "I'll see you again, somehow," he whimpered. Tears welled up in his eyes. They streamed down his face as he turned away.

The rumbling continued. There was no time to mourn. The rest of the building was about to cave in. Zane raced up the stairs, out of Snaxtime, and escaped the crumbling structure.

He ran through the parking lot and across the street before looking back. The building collapsed inward with a loud, forceful implosion. The boom sent up a cloud of dust and debris, hiding the ruins of the beloved fast-food restaurant.

Zane felt the first raindrop on his cheek. The sky roared with thunder, and a sudden downpour cleansed his battered body.

He had banished the demon queen and saved the world in the process. But the cost was high.

Zane thought about Dexter—the friend who always made everybody laugh, even when he was struggling the most. But Zane knew that Dexter was stronger and smarter than he ever gave himself credit for. His humor, it turned out, had been the glue holding them all together. He was irreplaceable.

And then there was Jake, who was larger than life. He had a natural confidence, a magnetic energy that drew people to him. But beneath that bravado, Jake was always watching out for his friends, making sure everyone was smiling and having a good time. He was such a good guy.

Zane thought about the heartbreak of Star's betrayal. Despite her deception, losing her was still a tragedy. He remembered that summer night in the back of the truck when they almost kissed. She had been so sweet, and it felt like, in that moment, she really understood him. He was pretty sure she did. That memory, filled with possibilities that would never be realized, remained etched in his heart.

Maybe that was part of the journey, too. Learning to hold onto the good even when everything else fell apart.

Hunter. He was more than a protector. He awakened something in Zane that had been hidden deep inside. Zane looked down at his ring. The stone was dull and lifeless.

Then, just ahead, he saw his skateboard in the middle of the street, as if it had been waiting for him.

With a weary smile, he hobbled over, stepped on, and let its wheels carry him away. Wet and weak, he skated off as sirens grew louder in the distance.

A new beginning awaited him.

But first things first.

He sure was hungry.

EPILOGUE

"Order's up, girls!" The cook rang the bell with urgency.

The kitchen at Pizza Princess was slammed. Perched atop a hill with a view of Paradise Falls, the VIP nightclub and pizza restaurant had become the town's hottest sensation since opening a few weeks ago.

Three waitresses in skimpy uniforms were huddled near the soda fountain, gossiping about the latest drama in their lives. It was obvious they were hired more for their looks than their work ethic. One of them, a blonde with an easy smile, grabbed a pizza from the counter and strutted out of the kitchen, balancing the tray on one hand.

The other two continued chatting, their conversation drifting from last night's party to the hot bartender's tattoos. The kitchen door swung open, and a new girl walked in, already in uniform. She was chewing gum and had a short red pixie cut.

"Oh my God, so cute," one of the waitresses said while looking her up and down. "Love the hair."

"Hey, girls," the new girl said with a lazy wave.

"Welcome to Pizza Princess," the other waitress said. "I hope you're ready—it's a jungle out there."

"Yeah, it gets *sooo* busy," the first girl added. "This place is, like, literally Hell. Survive a week, and *maybe* we'll be impressed."

"Oh, I'm not worried," the redhead proclaimed. "I can handle it."

"So, you've worked at a place like this before?"

The new girl shrugged. "Yeah, and I think I'm gonna settle in just fine. In fact, I have big plans for this place." She pulled an old book out of her bag. "I brought a few fun recipes to try out. Who's ready to cook up some trouble?"

The other waitresses exchanged curious glances. The new girl's confidence was intriguing.

"So, what's your name anyway?" one of them finally asked.

She extended her hand, her cherry-red nails gleaming like candies. "I'm Starling. The pleasure is totally *yours*."

ABOUT THE AUTHOR

J.J. Buffet is the joint pen name of Snaxtime, the Brooklyn-based creative team behind offbeat animations like CHEESE DOG: THE MOVIE and the cult-favorite viral horror short PIZZA FACE. With DEMON SUMMER, their spooky and fun debut novel, Snaxtime expands into new storytelling territory, bringing their signature blend of dark humor and imaginative flair to the page for the first time.

Web: snaxtime.com
Instagram: @snaxtimeusa
YouTube: @snaxtime